A RAVAGED SKIES NOVEL

WASTED WORLD

DJ COOPER

Find DJ Cooper on the web.

Https://AuthoroftheApocalypse.com

Don't forget to sign up for the spam free newsletter

https://bit.ly/3KmAGjh

"The world breaks everyone, and afterward, many are strong at the broken places."

—Ernest Hemingway

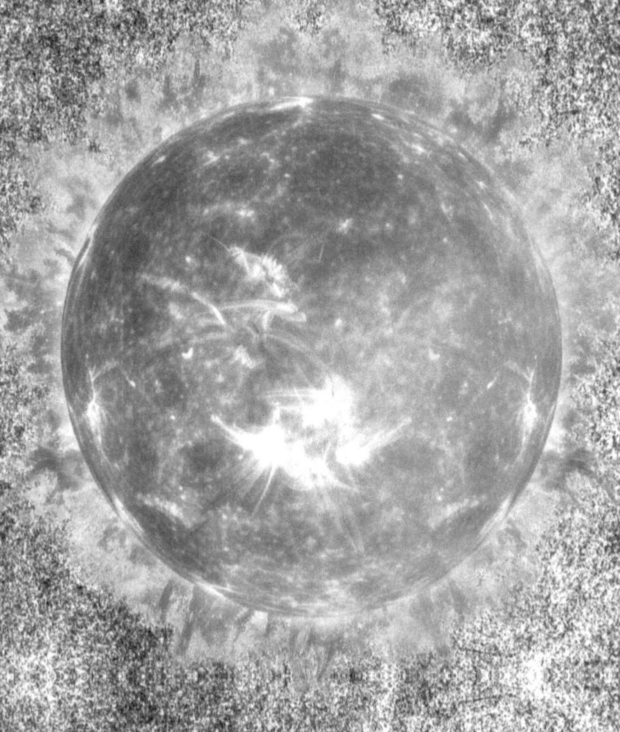

"THIS IS THE WAY THE WORLD ENDS
THIS IS THE WAY THE WORLD ENDS
THIS IS THE WAY THE WORLD ENDS
NOT WITH A BANG BUT A WHIMPER."
—T.S. ELIOT

Harvard University—July 12th

THE JULY SUN BLAZED ACROSS HARVARD YARD, THE heat shimmering off ancient brick pathways like a living mirage. Maddie Foster adjusted her designer sunglasses, the tortoiseshell frames catching the light as she twisted a strand of her chestnut hair. "I can't believe we're actually here," she said, her voice bubbling with a mix of excitement and disbelief.

Hannah Mitchell bumped her playfully, the movement causing her lightweight summer tank to shift off one shoulder. "I know, right? After all those late nights studying, all those practice tests—" She dramatically rolled her eyes. "Grace, stop bouncing. You're going to trip."

Grace Reynolds, the youngest of the trio, was literally skipping between the historic brick buildings, her energy impossible to contain. "I can't help it!" she practically sang, her bright blue sneakers dancing across the pathways. "This is Harvard. HARVARD!" She spun around, her strawberry-blonde ponytail whipping through the air. "I'm the first in my family to even visit an Ivy League campus, let alone potentially attend one."

Maddie laughed, the sound amused but warm. The

afternoon was scorching—mid-July heat pressing down with relentless intensity. The campus smelled of sun-baked stone, fresh-cut grass, and that indefinable scent of possibility. Coffee from a nearby café wafted between the historic buildings, competing with the soft buzz of cicadas hidden in the trees.

"We should get a group selfie by that statue," Hannah suggested, pointing toward a bronze figure partially obscured by elm trees. "Something to make my little brother totally jealous."

Grace was already pulling out her phone, her fingers dancing with excitement. "Totally. He thinks I'm just—"

The world around them changed.

It wasn't a dramatic explosion of light, but a subtle, unsettling shift. The air began to tingle—not with brightness, but with an electromagnetic pulse that made the hair on Maddie's arms stand on end. Her phone—poised to take the selfie—flickered, the screen going dark with a soft, electronic whisper.

Something felt wrong. The cicadas fell silent. The air seemed to compress, then expand, carrying a low, almost imperceptible hum that vibrated through their bones. The sky didn't change color dramatically, but took on a strange, muted quality—as if someone had slightly desaturated the world around them.

"Do you feel that?" Hannah whispered, her typically confident voice suddenly small.

Grace's phone died in her hand, the screen going black without warning. The summer heat seemed to pause, suspended in a moment of unnatural stillness.

They moved as a cluster, their earlier excitement replaced

by a nervous, uncertain energy. The campus, moments ago so vibrant and alive, now felt eerily silent. Occasional bursts of static electricity made Maddie's hair stand on end. What felt like tiny sparks danced between her fingers when she smoothed it.

"Something's wrong," Hannah muttered, her voice tight. She pulled out her now-dead phone, repeatedly pressing the power button. "No signal. Nothing. This can't be happening."

Maddie was scanning the grounds, her usual composure fracturing. "Look," she said, pointing to a group of people near the library steps. "Maybe they'll know something."

But as they approached, they realized the small cluster was in equal chaos. A professor in khaki shorts and a rumpled button-down was arguing with a maintenance worker, their voices rising with frustration. "—can't communicate with anyone!" the professor was saying, his face red and sweating in the July heat.

Grace's breathing became shallow. "My internship application," she whispered, a note of panic creeping into her voice. "I was supposed to confirm details today. My laptop, my phone—everything's dead."

A few students wandered past, looking confused. One girl was crying silently, her mascara streaking down her cheeks. Another group huddled together, speaking in hushed, urgent tones.

The electromagnetic charge continued to pulse through the air, creating an invisible tension that made their skin crawl. Hannah reached out, gripping Maddie's arm. "This isn't normal," she said. "Something's seriously wrong."

As they stood frozen, trying to make sense of their surroundings, a sudden commotion erupted. A man—dressed in running gear, his face wild with fear—came barreling down the pathway. His eyes were unfocused, his movements erratic, and showed no signs of stopping.

"Watch out!" Maddie tried to call, but it was too late.

The runner slammed into their group, his momentum sending Grace flying. She hit the ground hard, a sharp cry of pain escaping her lips as her body crashed against the ancient brick pathway. The man didn't stop, didn't even look back, just continued running as if something terrifying was chasing him.

Hannah and Maddie stood frozen for a moment, shock written across their faces. Grace lay on the ground, her mint green sneakers askew, a thin trickle of blood forming where her elbow had scraped against the unforgiving brick.

The silence of the Harvard Yard was now punctuated only by Grace's ragged breathing and the distant, incomprehensible sounds of mounting confusion.

Hannah was the first to move, dropping to her knees beside Grace. "Oh my God, oh my God," she repeated, her hands hovering uncertainly over her friend. Maddie crouched down, her designer sunglasses now pushed up into her hair, revealing eyes wide with a mixture of shock and growing fear.

"Grace?" Maddie's voice cracked. "Can you hear me?"

Grace blinked, dazed. A thin line of blood traced her elbow where it had struck the brick, and her mint green sneaker was now scuffed and dirty. "What… what just happened?" she mumbled, trying to sit up.

Hannah helped her, her movements jerky and nervous. "Some guy just ran into you. Didn't even stop." She looked around, and for the first time, Maddie noticed how Hannah's hands were shaking.

"We need to find help," Maddie said, but her voice lacked conviction. The campus, usually bustling with summer programs and tours, now felt like a ghost town. A few scattered people moved in the distance, but they seemed lost, disoriented. No one was running normal campus activities. No one was doing anything normal at all.

Grace finally managed to sit up fully, wincing. "My phone," she said suddenly. "My laptop. My entire life is digital. How am I supposed to—" Her voice caught, and Maddie recognized the pre-cry hiccup that meant a breakdown was imminent.

"Hey," Maddie said firmly, dropping down to eye level with Grace. "We're going to figure this out. Together."

But even as she said the words, she didn't believe them. The strange electric charge in the air, the dead electronics, the panicked runner—nothing made sense. And the silence. The unnatural, pressing silence was the worst part.

A distant siren began to wail.

Then another.

Then another.

James

The day before—Cornish, Maine

EVENING NEWS FLICKERED ON THE WIDESCREEN television, casting a bluish light across James Thompson's living room. Sarah sat beside him, her feet tucked under a well-worn throw blanket, absently twirling a strand of her graying hair.

"Another solar storm," the meteorologist was saying, his graphic showing an angry, mottled sun. "These sunspots are becoming quite the conversation piece."

James leaned forward, taking a swig of his beer. "You hear that?" he said to Sarah, more conversational than concerned. "Crazy how something happening millions of miles away could just… mess everything up down here."

The newscaster continued, describing potential disruptions. "Satellites could go dark, power grids might flicker," he was saying. "But hey, silver lining? Some spectacular aurora displays are expected."

"Wouldn't mind seeing that," James mused. "Beats another night of reruns."

The sliding glass door opened, and Matthew—all six-foot-two of him—walked in, his girlfriend Elena's hand intertwined with his. Her pregnancy was now unmistakable, a gentle curve beneath a light summer top.

"Hey Mom, Dad," Matthew called out. Elena waved, her other hand resting on her growing belly.

"We're thinking of heading to the beach tomorrow," Matthew said, settling onto the arm of his mother's chair and giving her a quick kiss on the cheek. "Heard these solar storms might make for some incredible light shows. Elena's never seen the aurora."

Sarah smiled. "Sounds romantic. Just be careful with all this solar activity they're talking about."

James chuckled. "Careful of what? Some lights in the sky?"

"Stay for dinner?" Sarah asked, already moving toward the kitchen. "I've got a lasagna that'll be perfect."

Elena's face lit up. "Oh, I'd love to! I've been craving your lasagna for weeks." She rubbed her belly, a gesture that had become as natural as breathing. "This little one seems to have inherited my love for your cooking."

Matthew grinned. "And my appetite, clearly."

Sarah pulled out a cutting board, her movements practiced and familiar. "How's the pregnancy going? Any new updates?"

"We have an ultrasound next week," Elena said, her excitement bubbling over. "We're hoping to find out the sex. I'm thinking it's a girl—Matthew thinks boy, of course."

James and Matthew drifted toward the back patio, beers in hand. "So, that interview?" James prompted.

"Tech startup," Matthew explained. "Software development position. Competitive package, good growth potential." He took a swig of his beer. "Fingers crossed."

Back in the kitchen, they could hear Sarah still chatting

with Elena, already deep in baby shower planning mode. "I'm thinking light yellow for the theme. Gender-neutral, but still warm. But once we know, that could change. What do you think?"

Elena nodded enthusiastically. "I love that idea. They said it is not always evident this early."

In the background, the television continued its indistinct murmur about solar activity, a subtle reminder of the approaching event.

A sharp knock interrupted the family's comfortable chatter.

"James, can you get that?" Sarah called from the kitchen, where she was pulling the lasagna from the oven.

James trudged to the door, already sensing something was different about this interruption. He pulled it open to find Old Man Jenkins—local retired meteorologist and town conspiracy theorist—standing on the porch. Jenkins was more disheveled than usual, his white hair wild and his eyes intense behind thick glasses.

"Thompson," Jenkins said without preamble, "we need to talk about what's coming."

James sighed. Jenkins was known for his dire predictions, most of which never amounted to anything more than hot air. "Everything okay, Jenkins?"

"Okay? OKAY?" Jenkins's voice rose, causing Matthew and Elena to exchange a glance from the living room. "That solar event—it's not just another storm. This is different. I've been tracking these sunspots. The magnetic configuration, the plasma density—it's unprecedented."

James tried to keep his tone light. "Want to come in? Sarah's just made lasagna."

Jenkins hesitated, then nodded sharply. His eyes darted around the room, taking in the family scene before focusing back on James with an urgency that suggested he had something critical to share.

As Jenkins entered, his agitation was palpable. Elena unconsciously moved closer to Matthew, her hand protectively resting on her belly. Sarah watched him warily from the kitchen, lasagna server suspended mid-air.

"The ham radio community," Jenkins began, his voice dropping to a conspiratorial whisper as he sat at the table, "they're talking. This isn't just another solar flare. We're looking at a potential catastrophic event."

Matthew tried to lighten the mood. "Another doomsday prediction, Mr. Jenkins?"

But Jenkins was undeterred. His hands, weathered and spotted with age, began to gesture wildly. "I've got contacts from Alaska to Florida. Operators are reporting strange electromagnetic readings. The sun's behaving in ways we've never seen before."

Sarah placed the lasagna on the table, her movements slow and deliberate. "Would you like some dinner, Mr. Jenkins?"

"I need you to listen," Jenkins said to James, leaning forward. His eyes were intense, almost feverish. "You're on the town council. Parks committee might seem small, but you've got connections. Someone needs to prepare."

Elena shifted uncomfortably. Matthew noticed and placed a reassuring hand on her knee.

"Prepare for what, exactly?" James asked, his tone measured but curious.

Jenkins lowered his voice. "Total communication

breakdown. Power grid collapse. Satellites falling from the sky." He looked around the table, his gaze lingering on Elena's pregnant belly. "Civilization isn't as stable as we think."

The room fell silent, save for the low murmur of the television in the background, still reporting on solar activity.

Jenkins picked up his fork, took a massive bite of lasagna, and his entire demeanor transformed. "Good Lord, Sarah," he mumbled through a mouthful of pasta, "best lasagna in three counties. James, you snagged yourself a real treasure years ago." He winked at Elena. "Mark my words, young lady, find yourself a man who appreciates a good cook."

The tension momentarily dissolved into laughter. Sarah blushed, a hint of her younger self showing through.

But just as quickly, Jenkins' mood darkened. He set down his fork, lasagna momentarily forgotten. "After a massive CME? We're talking about potential societal collapse. No power grid means no communications. No internet. No cell towers. Imagine a world where everything electronic simply… dies."

His hands started moving again, painting a grim picture. "Hospitals running on emergency generators. Food supply chains disrupted. No refrigeration. No ATMs. People will realize how dependent we are on technology in about 48 hours."

Matthew leaned forward, genuinely intrigued now. "You really think it could be that bad?"

"Bad?" Jenkins scoffed. "We're talking about potentially sending us back to the stone age. One massive electromagnetic pulse, and civilization's infrastructure could be crippled for months. Maybe years."

James leaned back, his fork hovering over his plate.

"You're talking about a worst-case scenario, right? These solar events happen all the time."

"Not like this," Jenkins insisted. "The last time we saw something remotely similar was the 1859 Carrington Event. Telegraphs failed worldwide. Some operators reported sparks flying from their equipment." He looked around the table, his eyes intense. "Imagine that, but with our entire digital infrastructure."

Elena, who had been quiet, spoke up. "What about medical equipment? My pregnancy—"

Jenkins softened momentarily. "Hospitals have backup systems. Generators. But long-term? Supply chains for medications, medical supplies—all dependent on digital communication."

Matthew chimed in, his tech background surfacing. "Cloud servers would go down. Banking systems. Transportation networks rely on GPS, satellite communications."

"Precisely," Jenkins nodded. "One massive solar punch, and we're talking about a global reset. No phone. No internet. No way to quickly communicate or coordinate."

Sarah, who had been listening quietly, finally spoke. "How likely is this, really?"

Jenkins took another bite of lasagna, chewing thoughtfully. "Probability's low. But the potential impact? Catastrophic."

The room fell silent, the weight of his words hanging in the air like an unspoken threat.

Maddie

Harvard University Campus

A UNIVERSITY ADMINISTRATOR CLIMBED THE STEPS of University Hall, his crisp white shirt now damp with sweat, a megaphone clutched in his trembling hand. The crowd—a mixture of summer program students, campus workers, and confused tourists—fell silent.

"Attention everyone," he called out, his voice crackling with tension. "All campus activities are immediately suspended. The power outage is not localized to Harvard—it appears to be widespread. We cannot confirm the extent of the disruption at this time. All visitors are advised to seek alternative transportation and local shelter."

Hannah turned to Maddie and Grace, her face pale. "We came down on the Downeaster from Portland. How are we supposed to get back?"

Grace, still nursing a bruised elbow from her earlier fall, looked around nervously. "Our train tickets are digital. My phone's dead. How do we even prove we have reservations?"

Maddie was already taking charge, her practical nature emerging. "We'll walk to North Station. It's not that far— maybe two miles. We can figure out tickets when we get there." She adjusted her bag, checking that their essential items were secure. "We've got some cash. Worst case, we buy new tickets."

"Walk?" Hannah's voice rose slightly. "In this heat? With everything going crazy?"

"We don't have many options," Maddie said firmly. She helped Grace to her feet, noticing how the younger girl was still slightly unsteady. "We stick together. Stay close."

The campus, usually bustling with summer energy, now felt eerily quiet. Small clusters of people moved hesitantly, like actors unsure of their marks. The oppressive July heat seemed to amplify the sense of uncertainty.

"At least we're together," Grace offered, trying to sound optimistic. But her voice trembled slightly, betraying the fear beneath her words.

They moved as a tight cluster, navigating the Harvard campus with increasing unease. The streets that had been bustling with summer tour groups and students were now eerily quiet, punctuated only by occasional confused murmurs and the distant sound of sirens.

Grace walked between Maddie and Hannah, her earlier excitement completely replaced by a growing sense of anxiety. "I can't believe this is happening," she muttered, rubbing her bruised elbow. "My internship application, my phone, everything—just gone."

Hannah kept glancing around, her normally confident stride now tentative. "Something's seriously wrong. I've never seen Boston so subdued."

Hannah led the way, her navigation skills kicking in. She'd grown up in Portland and knew how to read maps, even without digital assistance. "North Station is about two miles. We'll cut through Harvard Square, then down towards the Charles River."

Small groups of people moved erratically around them. A professor argued with a campus security guard. A group of international students huddled together, speaking in rapid, worried tones. The electromagnetic charge still hung in the air, making their skin prickle with an unsettling static electricity.

"We should have water," Maddie said, scanning a small convenience store they were passing. The windows were open, the electronic payment systems clearly non-functional. "Hannah, you've got cash, right?"

Hannah nodded, pulling a twenty-dollar bill from her wallet. "Let's hope they'll take cash."

The convenience store was dim, sunlight filtering through windows that seemed more like portals to an alternate reality. A heavy-set man stood behind the counter, his eyes darting nervously between the three young women and the door.

"Five dollars a bottle," he said flatly, placing three water bottles on the counter.

Maddie's jaw clenched. "Excuse me?"

"Power's out. Supply chains are down. Water's a premium now." His voice was matter-of-fact, almost challenging.

A quick memory flashed through Maddie's mind—Old Man Jenkins, his wild eyes, talking about societal collapse. Something about infrastructure falling apart, people turning desperate. She remembered his words about how quickly civilization could unravel.

Nahhh, she thought. Can't be.

"These price signs clearly show these water bottles are $2.50," Maddie said, pointing to a faded poster near the refrigerator. "And these protein bars are $1.50 each."

The cashier shifted, his bulk blocking the narrow aisle. "Different rules now. Supply and demand."

Hannah stepped forward, her hand on Maddie's arm. Grace hung back, looking small and worried.

"Twenty dollars," Maddie negotiated. "Three waters. Three protein bars. That's fair."

A tense moment passed. The cashier's eyes narrowed, then he nodded abruptly. "Fine."

As they walked out, water bottles clutched tightly, Grace whispered, "Why was he so… weird?"

Maddie didn't answer immediately. The electromagnetic charge still hung in the air, making her skin prickle with an unsettling sense that all of this was very wrong.

As they approached North Station, the normally bustling transportation hub looked like a scene from a half-abandoned movie set. Clusters of people stood in confused groups, some with suitcases, others simply staring at dead electronic displays. The usual hum of announcements and electronic screens was replaced by a low, anxious murmur.

"The trains won't be running," an older woman muttered to no one in particular. "No power means no signals. No way to control the tracks."

Maddie scanned the area, her hand unconsciously moving closer to Hannah and Grace. A group of young men near a broken vending machine were sizing up its contents, their body language tense and predatory. One of them had a tire iron, casually held at his side—not quite threatening, but not innocent either.

The July heat made everything feel more claustrophobic. Sweat traced lines down necks, clothes already beginning to stick. The station's large windows allowed sunlight to pour in, but the usual brightness felt oppressive, highlighting the growing tension.

"We need a plan," Hannah whispered, her eyes darting between the potential troublemakers and the station's main entrance. "We can't stay here."

Grace pressed closer to her friends, her earlier excitement about Harvard completely forgotten. The bruise on her elbow throbbed, a physical reminder of how quickly things had changed.

Maddie guided them to a quieter corner near a large area map, positioning herself so they could see both the map and the station's main area. A couple nearby caught their attention.

"—massive coronal mass ejection," a man was saying to his companion. "Worse than anything we've seen in decades. Satellite communications are completely down."

Hannah leaned in close, her voice a hushed whisper. "We can't stay here after dark. Boston gets dangerous fast when things break down." She traced a line on the map with her finger. "We're about two miles from the coast. If we can't get transport, we might need to start walking."

Grace looked pale. "Walking? To where?"

Maddie's mind drifted back to Portland, to Old Man Jenkins and his wild-eyed warnings. "You know," she muttered, "Jenkins was talking about something like this. Always going on about solar storms and infrastructure collapse." She shook her head. "Always seemed like a conspiracy nut. But now"

"But now what?" Hannah pressed.

The group of young men had shifted, their attention

occasionally sliding toward the three women. Not overtly threatening, but definitely calculating.

"We need a plan," Maddie said firmly. "Something that keeps us together and keeps us moving." She studied the map. "There are suburbs north of the city. Maybe we can find transport. Or at least somewhere safer than this station."

Grace's hand unconsciously went to her bruised elbow. "Those guys are watching us," she whispered.

Hannah's jaw set. "I know. We need to look confident. Prepared. Not like easy targets."

Maddie deliberately raised her voice, just loud enough to carry. "Hannah, your cousin Jason's place is only a mile north, right? You think he'll let us crash there tonight?"

"Hells yeah," Hannah said catching on instantly, "they're a cool bunch of guys. They like their football and bachelor pad, but they'd totally let us."

Grace's ears perked up. "Wait, how many guys live there?"

Hannah caught Maddie's eye before making something up. "Four roommates," she said smoothly, adding a strategic wink.

Grace's demeanor instantly transformed. "Four cute guys?" Her earlier fear momentarily replaced by teenage excitement.

The summer heat pressed against them, thick and oppressive. Sweat traced delicate lines down Maddie's neck, her L.L. Bean tank top was already damp. She caught a quick glance from one of the guys near the vending machine—tall, dark hair. Definitely knew he was attractive.

"Those guys think they're all that," she murmured to Hannah, a mix of dismissal and mild interest in her voice.

Hannah's eyes darted sideways. "Totally. But they're

watching us like we're prey." Her hand instinctively moved closer to Grace, protective.

The young men's attention seemed to shift, their predatory energy momentarily diverted by the hint of potential interaction elsewhere.

Maddie led the way as they made for the door at the other end of the terminal with Grace continuing her excitement at the potential for meeting some new guys working into the ploy to make them less of a target but completely annoying at how she could be so clueless. A growing sense of unease rose that Maddie couldn't shake. A hint of terror rolled up her spine sending a shiver through her body in spite of the heavy July heat.

The Callahan Tunnel loomed before them like a maw, its entrance a throat of absolute darkness that swallowed the fading daylight. A few abandoned cars sat at odd angles, their headlights still burning—the batteries not yet dead—creating long, twisted shadows that danced along the tunnel's curved walls. The July heat seemed to intensify in the enclosed space, mixing with the acrid smell of exhaust, burned rubber, and something else—something metallic and wet that made Maddie's stomach turn.

"We can't," Grace whispered, her fingers digging into Maddie's arm. "Please, we can't go in there. There has to be another way around."

Hannah's voice shook slightly as she wiped sweat from her forehead. "The bridges are chaos. People fighting, jumping off cars… This is our best shot at getting north."

A distant scream echoed from somewhere behind them, followed by the sound of breaking glass. The city was growing more violent by the hour.

"Okay," Maddie breathed, trying to sound more confident than she felt. "Okay. We stay close. Grace between us. Count steps if you have to, just keep moving."

They entered the tunnel slowly, the temperature dropping noticeably as darkness enveloped them. Their footsteps echoed wetly against the concrete, and something crunched beneath their feet—broken glass maybe, or worse. The few working headlights created islands of harsh brightness that made the darkness between them seem absolute. Their shadows stretched and distorted along the curved walls, multiplying and overlapping until it seemed like a crowd of dark figures walked with them.

The smell grew worse as they moved deeper—stagnant air thick with exhaust fumes, whatever else from the abandoned vehicles, and that metallic tang that reminded Maddie of pennies in her mouth. Water dripped somewhere in the darkness, each drop echoing like a gunshot.

Grace's breathing became increasingly erratic, short gasps that seemed too loud in the enclosed space. "I can't—I can't see—I can't breathe—"

"Shh," Hannah whispered, but her own voice trembled. "Just hold onto me. One foot in front of the other."

They passed a minivan, its driver's door hanging open. A child's car seat was visible in the glow of the dashboard lights, empty except for a small stuffed rabbit dropped on the floor. Grace made a choking sound.

Something skittered in the darkness ahead—rats maybe, or just debris shifting in the tunnel's strange air currents. Grace stumbled, her sandal catching on something unseen. She went down hard, dragging Maddie with her. The ground was wet beneath their hands.

"Don't think about it," Hannah hissed, helping them up. "Just keep moving."

A sharp crash somewhere ahead made them freeze. Grace's fingers dug painfully into Maddie's arm as voices drifted through the darkness—male voices, laughing about something. The sound bounced off the walls, multiplying until it seemed to come from everywhere at once.

"Here," Maddie breathed, barely a whisper, tugging them toward a recessed maintenance door. The handle wouldn't turn—locked—but the alcove provided some cover. They pressed themselves into the shallow space, trying to control their breathing as the voices grew closer.

"—checking every car," a deep voice echoed. "Bound to find something good."

"Found these in the last one," another voice answered, followed by the sound of pills rattling in bottles. "Rich people and their prescriptions, man."

Grace started hyperventilating, each breath seemingly louder than the last. Hannah pressed her hand over Grace's mouth, but a small sound had already escaped—a whimper that bounced between the curved walls.

The laughter stopped.

"The fuck was that?"

Footsteps approached—three sets, maybe four. Impossible to tell with the echoes. A flashlight beam cut through the darkness, sweeping back and forth. Maddie pressed herself harder against the cold concrete, feeling Grace trembling violently between them.

"Come on out," a voice called, closer now. "We just want to talk."

The flashlight beam passed over their alcove—once, twice. Maddie held her breath, heart thundering so loud she was sure they would hear it. Grace's tears were hot against her shoulder.

"There!"

The beam caught them full in the face, momentarily blinding. Grace screamed—a high, terrified sound that shattered the tunnel's strange silence.

"Run!" Maddie shoved Grace forward, out of the alcove. They bolted into darkness, shoes slipping on the wet concrete. The flashlight beam danced crazily around them as shouts echoed off the walls. Something crashed behind them—metal on concrete—followed by cursing.

They ran blind through the alternating patches of headlight brightness and absolute darkness. Grace stumbled again, sprawling forward. Hannah caught her arm but lost her own balance, both of them going down hard. Maddie turned back, trying to help them up as footsteps thundered closer.

"Split up!" A voice called. "Cut them off at the exit!"

The beam of light found them again. Hannah was bleeding from her knee, Grace crying openly now. Maddie yanked them both up, ignoring Grace's cry of pain.

"There!" Another maintenance door, this one slightly ajar. They squeezed through the gap into absolute darkness, pressing themselves against cold, damp walls. The space was tiny— some kind of electrical closet—forcing them to stand pressed together. The smell of mold and rust filled their lungs.

Footsteps pounded past their hiding place. Voices called back and forth, echoing impossibly: "Where'd they go?" "Check the alcoves!"

"They're here somewhere!"

Grace's entire body shook with silent sobs. Hannah's blood felt warm where it soaked through Maddie's shirt. They stood frozen, hardly daring to breathe as more footsteps approached—slower now, searching.

A shadow passed in front of the door's gap. Stopped. The beam of the flashlight played across the door's surface.

"This one's open."

Maddie's hand found a piece of pipe on the floor—rusted, heavy. Her fingers closed around it as the door began to move.

The screech of tires echoed through the tunnel—loud, close. Engines revving. New voices shouting.

"Shit! Cops!"

"Go, go, go!"

The footsteps retreated quickly, sounds of running fading into the tunnel's strange acoustics. Still, they waited—seconds stretching into minutes—before Maddie dared to peek out. The tunnel seemed empty except for the ever-present glow of abandoned headlights.

"We have to move," she whispered. "Now. Before they come back."

They emerged from the closet on shaking legs. Hannah limped slightly, blood trickling down her shin. Grace had lost one of her sandals somewhere in the chaos.

They moved as quickly as they dared through the remaining length of the tunnel, jumping at every echo, every drip of water, every shift of shadow. The exit, when it finally appeared, looked like salvation—a rectangle of natural light that seemed impossibly bright for the time of day after the tunnel's darkness.

They didn't stop running until they were several blocks

away, the tunnel's entrance no longer visible behind them. Grace collapsed against a storefront, her legs giving out completely. She'd run barefoot since losing her other sandal, and her feet were cut and bleeding. Hannah sat heavily beside her, examining her own bloodied knee.

Maddie stood guard, still clutching the rusted pipe, scanning their surroundings. Her heart wouldn't stop racing, and every sound made her flinch. The aurora danced overhead, painting everything in strange colors, but after the tunnel's darkness, even its alien light felt reassuring.

"We can't—" Grace choked out between sobs, "we can't do that again. Please. Please don't make us do that again."

"We won't have to," Hannah said, her medical training kicking in as she examined Grace's feet. "But we need to clean these cuts. Find somewhere to rest."

Maddie watched smoke rise from various points across the city, her hands still shaking around the piece of pipe she couldn't make herself let go of. The tunnel had been terrifying, but at least its dangers had been contained, defined. Out here, under the impossible aurora, anything could be waiting.

"Five minutes," she said quietly, forcing authority into her voice despite her trembling. "Then we keep moving. We need to find shelter before dark."

Grace just sobbed harder, curling into herself on the dirty sidewalk. Hannah met Maddie's eyes over Grace's huddled form, and Maddie saw her own terror reflected there. They were alive, but the darkness of the tunnel had changed something in all of them.

The city burned around them as the aurora painted everything in its otherworldly light, and somewhere in the distance, more screams echoed off brick and concrete.

James

The day—Cornish, Maine

JAMES THOMPSON STOOD AT HIS KITCHEN WINDOW, coffee mug warming his weathered hands, watching the strange shimmer in the morning sky. The colors seemed brighter and Jenkins' words from the night before kept echoing in his mind: *"This isn't just another solar flare. We're looking at a potential catastrophic event."*

"Sarah?" he called out, not taking his eyes off the horizon. "Have you noticed anything… odd about the sky this morning?"

Sarah barely glanced up from her notebook where she was scribbling baby shower ideas. "Hmm? Oh, James, do you think yellow is too generic for the theme? Elena mentioned she loves yellow, but maybe we should wait until we know if it's a boy or girl."

"Sarah." His voice carried more weight this time. "About what Jenkins said last night—"

"James Thompson, don't you dare." Sarah's pen stopped moving. "That man has predicted everything from alien invasions to government conspiracies. I won't have him ruining Elena's first baby shower with his doom and gloom."

James turned from the window, studying his wife. Sarah sat

at their worn kitchen table, surrounded by magazine clippings and color swatches. Her reading glasses had slipped down her nose, and she pushed them back up with familiar irritation. The morning sun caught the silver in her hair—when had there gotten to be so much of it?

"He showed me the data," James said quietly. "Real measurements from his equipment. And the ham radio community—"

"The ham radio community," Sarah echoed with a dismissive wave. "A bunch of old men playing with their toys. James, we have real things to worry about. Elena's appointment is next week, and I need to coordinate with her mother about the guest list."

The coffee in James' mug had grown cold. Outside, the sky's strange shimmer intensified, though Sarah seemed determined not to notice. His mind went to the generator in the barn, the stockpile of fuel he'd maintained out of habit. Maybe it was time to check those supplies.

"I'm going to town," he said finally. "Need to talk to Jenkins again, maybe stop by Foster's Hardware."

Sarah's pen scratched against paper. "While you're there, could you pick up some yellow cardstock? I'm thinking of making the invitations myself. More personal that way."

James set his mug down and moved behind his wife, placing his hands on her shoulders. She stiffened slightly but didn't pull away. "Sarah," he said softly, "I know you're excited about the baby. I am, too. But something's coming. Something big. And we need to be ready."

For just a moment, Sarah's hand trembled over her notebook. Then she straightened, shrugging off his touch. "The only thing coming is our first grandchild, James. And I won't let Old Man Jenkins' paranoid fantasies overshadow that."

James opened his mouth to argue further, but the lights flickered—just once, barely noticeable. Sarah didn't seem to register it, but James felt his stomach tighten. He grabbed his keys from the hook by the door.

"I'll be back soon," he said.

Sarah was already back to her planning. "Don't forget the cardstock. And James? Maybe get some blue and pink. too. Just in case."

As he stepped outside, the morning air felt charged, like the moment before a thunderstorm. But the sky above held no clouds—just that strange coloring that reminded him of just before a storm. Smaller flares had affected things and even offered auroras earlier in the week and the news did say there could be minor cell and radio static and interruptions but Jenkins' words echoed again: *Civilization isn't as stable as we think.*

James climbed into his truck, the engine turning over with a familiar rumble. He needed to prepare, whether Sarah accepted it or not. The real question was: how much time did they have left?

The old Ford's engine hummed as James pulled onto the main road, his mind racing faster than the truck. He pulled out his cell phone—still working, still connected to a world that might not exist by nightfall. He dialed Emily first, knowing his daughter would be getting the kids ready for summer day camp.

"Dad?" Emily's voice crackled through the speaker. He could hear Sophia and Ethan squabbling in the background. "Everything okay? It's kind of early."

"Emily, honey, I need you to listen." He kept his voice

steady, measured. "Jenkins came by last night with some concerning information about these solar storms. I'm heading to his place now to—"

"Dad, seriously?" The eye-roll was audible in her voice. "Old Man Jenkins? The same guy who swore the government was controlling the weather with satellites?"

A burst of static cut through the line. James glanced at the sky—that ethereal shimmer was getting stronger.

"Emily, this is different. The data he showed me—"

"Hold on," she interrupted. "Ethan! Put your sister's backpack down right now!" There was a shuffling sound, then Michael's voice came on the line.

"James? Michael here. Sorry about that—morning chaos." His son-in-law's military training always showed in his precise way of speaking. "What's this about Jenkins?"

James explained quickly about Jenkins' measurements, the ham radio reports, the strange atmospheric readings. The line crackled with increasing static, but Michael listened without interruption.

"Electromagnetic pulse potential?" Michael asked sharply. "That tracks with some chatter I've been hearing. Meet you at Jenkins' place in twenty?"

"Make it thirty. Need to try Matthew first."

After hanging up, James immediately dialed his son. The call went straight to voicemail twice before connecting on the third try. Reception was definitely deteriorating.

"Dad?" Matthew sounded distracted. "Can I call you back? Elena's not feeling great this morning, and we've got that ultrasound appointment—"

"Matthew, listen." James cut him off, something he rarely

did. "I need you and Elena to—" Static cut out part of what he was trying to say.

"What? Dad? What did you say? Is this about Jenkins' visit? Mom texted me about it, said he was going on about some solar storm?"

The shimmer in the sky pulsed, and James' truck radio emitted a burst of static so loud he flinched.

"Did you hear that?" James asked.

"Yeah, weird. Look, Dad, I've got to—"

"Matthew." James rarely used this tone with his children—the one that brooked no argument. "Your mother's planning a baby shower. I'm planning for survival. One of us is reading this situation wrong, and I pray it's me. But if it's not, I need you to trust me right now."

The line went silent for so long James thought they'd lost connection. Finally, Matthew spoke, his voice smaller, younger somehow. "Okay, Dad. What do you need me to do?"

James could see Jenkins' property up ahead—the array of antennas and satellite dishes making it unmistakable. Michael's truck was already turning into the gravel driveway.

"Get Elena, get her medications, get anything important, and meet me at Jenkins' place. And Matthew? Hurry."

The call ended with another burst of static. James pulled in behind Michael's truck, noting how his son-in-law was already deep in conversation with Jenkins, both men gesturing at the equipment arrays. The morning sun cast long shadows through the strange aurora, and James couldn't shake the feeling that they were running out of time.

James cut the engine, the sudden silence making the strange static charge in the air more noticeable, almost like just before lightning struck. He strode toward Jenkins, hand outstretched. "Jenkins. Looks like I owe you an apology for not taking this more seriously last night."

Jenkins grasped his hand, but his usual firm grip was distracted, his eyes constantly darting to the equipment behind him. "No time for that now, Thompson. No time at all." He pulled a crumpled piece of paper from his pocket, hands trembling slightly. "Been monitoring the readings all morning. It's worse than I thought."

Michael stepped forward, his military bearing a stark contrast to Jenkins' nervous energy. "I told Emily to keep the kids home. She wasn't happy, but she'll listen." He glanced at the shimmering sky. "What's our timeline looking like?"

"Hours. Maybe less." Jenkins led them toward his garage, talking in fragmented bursts. "Need to protect your electronics. Anything with a circuit board. Metal trash cans—galvanized. Line them with cardboard. No metal-to-metal contact." His hands moved constantly, illustrating his words. "Layer it. Wrap things in foil first. Then cardboard. Then the can."

James watched as Jenkins yanked open his garage door, revealing shelves of meticulously organized equipment. "Got my whole house shielded. Copper mesh in the walls. But still got backups." He pointed to a row of metal trash cans. "Triple-layered Faraday cages. One fails, got two more."

"What should we prioritize?" Michael asked, already taking notes on his phone.

"Generators. Small electronics. Radio equipment." Jenkins' voice grew more urgent. "Medical devices—your Elena's pregnancy monitor, James. Car computers if you can. Modern vehicles'll be bricks without their electronics."

The sky pulsed with another wave of aurora, visible even

in the morning light. All three men looked up, and Jenkins' face went pale.

"Not good. Not good at all." He hurried to a bank of equipment, fingers dancing over dials. "Getting readings like nothing I've seen. This isn't just a normal CME. This is…" He trailed off, shaking his head.

"How much time?" James asked quietly.

Jenkins looked at his watch, then back at the sky. "Hours. Maybe less." He repeated. "Sun's too active. Magnetometer's going crazy." He turned to them, his usual conspiracy theorist demeanor replaced by genuine fear. "Get what you need now. Get your families prepared. When this hits" He swallowed hard. "There won't be any warning. Just… nothing. Everything goes dark."

Michael was already on his phone, likely texting Emily. James thought of Sarah, still planning her baby shower, and Matthew, hopefully on his way.

The morning sun continued to rise, but the growing aurora made it look alien, wrong. They were running out of time, and James could feel it in his bones.

"Show us exactly how to build these Faraday cages," he said firmly. "Then we move fast."

Jenkins nodded, already reaching for supplies. "First thing: metal has to be galvanized. Has to be completely sealed. Any gap bigger than a millimeter…" He mimed an explosion with his hands. "And you'll need tools. The old kind. Manual. Because once this hits," He looked at the sky again, his voice dropping. "we're going back in time, gentlemen. Way back."

Matthew's truck pulled in hard, gravel spraying. He climbed out, his usual easy smile replaced with irritation.

"Alright, I'm here. Elena's not happy about missing the appointment, Dad."

"Matthew—" James started, but Jenkins cut him off, thrusting a metal trash can at the younger man.

"Your phone. Give it here. And any other electronics you've got." Jenkins' hands moved rapid-fire, already lining the can with cardboard. "That fancy watch too. Anything with a chip."

Matthew looked to his father for explanation, but Michael stepped in. "It's not a debate, Matt. Do it now, we'll explain later."

"This is crazy," Matthew muttered, but he started emptying his pockets. "Meanwhile, Danny's probably off on another 'business trip', not answering his phone like usual. But sure, I'm the one who has to drop everything because Old Man Jenkins says—"

"Enough!" James' voice cracked like a whip. The morning aurora cast strange shadows across his face as he stepped toward his youngest. "Your brother's choices are his own. Right now, I need you to trust me. Please." His voice softened on the last word. "Get Elena to the farm. Your mother will take care of her. Then come back and help us prepare."

Michael was already on his phone. "Em? Yeah, pack up the kids. Take some clothes, any medications… No, I'm serious. Head to your parents' farm… I know, but—" He walked a few steps away, his voice dropping as he tried to convince his wife.

"Dad," Matthew started, but James held up his hand.

"Son, I have never asked you to blindly trust me. But I am now. Please."

Something in his father's tone must have reached Matthew.

He nodded slowly, accepting the now-packed Faraday cage from Jenkins. "Elena's not going to like this."

"Tell her Sarah's working on the baby shower," Michael called over, having finished his call. "That'll help."

James pulled out his phone, noting the increasing static in the air. Sarah answered on the fourth ring.

"James? Did you get the cardstock?"

"Sarah, honey, the kids are coming over for dinner. All of them." He tried to keep his voice casual. "Maybe make that beef stew they all love?"

"Everyone? Oh, that's wonderful!" Her voice brightened immediately. "Elena can help me with the shower plans. But James, the cardstock—"

"I'll pick some up," he said quickly, catching Jenkins' frantic gesturing about time running out. "Yellow, pink, and blue. Got it."

"Perfect! And fresh bread from Miller's?"

"Of course." He swallowed hard, knowing the bread might be the least of their concerns by dinner time. "Love you."

"Love you too. Don't forget—"

"The cardstock. I know."

He hung up, turning to find Jenkins already packing more Faraday cages with essential equipment. Michael was making a list of supplies, his military training evident in his systematic approach.

"Matthew," James said firmly. "Get Elena to the farm. Then meet us at Foster's Hardware. We need to move fast."

Jenkins puttered around, mumbling to himself, and spun on them, saying, "Time's running out, gentlemen. Whatever you're going to do, do it now."

The urgency struck James like a hammer to his chest. 'Time is running out,' he said. What would that actually mean? James thanked him and hurried to the truck where Michael was already climbing inside and headed for the hardware store.

The store's bell chimed as they entered, David Foster looking up from his register and offering a nod. Within minutes, they'd filled carts with supplies—manual tools, first aid kits, batteries. Michael's military precision guided their selections while Matthew's restless energy had him constantly adding *one more thing*.

They rolled up to the counter where David stood eyeing their choices. He asked, "What kind of contraption you building out there at the farm now?"

James hesitated but looked at him sternly. "I know most think old man Jenkins is a little off with his radio stuff but I think his warnings this time would be best if heeded. He thinks this solar flare could cause some issues."

David swiped his card to pay for the items while Michael and Matthew loaded them into the truck. "James, you are not taking his doomspeak seriously are you? He's always predicting the end of the world." His arms flew up as he continued, "The sky is falling."

"Can't hurt to be prepared, right?" James asked.

"Seems like a waste of money to me," David scoffed, then smiled, "but I might just close early, thanks to you."

James reached out his hand to shake. David gripped it and his look changed when James said, "Better safe than dead."

Back at the farm, the afternoon sun cast long shadows across the barn as they worked. The animals seemed agitated, sensing something the humans were trying to ignore. James and Michael methodically stored feed and supplies while Matthew organized the Faraday cages Jenkins had helped them prepare.

The familiar ring of Sarah's dinner bell cut through the heavy summer air at exactly five o'clock. Some things never changed—dinner was dinner, and Sarah Thompson didn't believe in serving late.

"Wash up, all of you," she called from the back porch, ever the proper hostess.

The dining room was a snapshot of forced normalcy. Sarah had set her best tablecloth, the good china reserved for Sunday dinners. Elena sat beside Matthew, her hand occasionally drifting to her belly. Emily tried to settle Sophia and Ethan while Michael quietly checked his watch. The beef stew's rich aroma filled the air, fresh bread from Miller's still warm on the table.

"Pass the salt, please," Sarah said, as if this were any other family dinner.

James reached for the salt cellar, his eyes catching the clock on the wall. 5:15 PM.

The lights flickered once.

Sarah didn't pause in serving Ethan another helping of stew. Elena asked about the baby shower colors. Matthew reached for more bread.

The lights flickered again.

5:19 PM.

Everything went dark and James' eyes shifted to look at Michael and Matthew both reflecting his knowing expression. Jenkins had been right. God help them. He'd been right for once.

Lynnfield, Massachusetts—The Day 5:19pm

"DADDY, THE TV WENT OFF!" LILY'S VOICE CARRIED from the family room just as Daniel Thompson was loosening his tie. The markets had been strange today—unexplained satellite delays, odd fluctuations in trading systems. He'd left the office early, an uneasy feeling settling in his stomach.

"It's not just the TV, Princess. Power's out on the whole street." He moved to the window of their executive colonial, seeing the entire neighborhood had gone dark. His neighbor's Tesla sat silent in their circular driveway, its charging cycle interrupted.

Jessica emerged from their gourmet kitchen, a battery-powered lantern already in hand and prepared to set up. "The garage door won't open—I had to use the manual release to get in." She was still in her business casual, having returned early from her real estate showings when her tablet started malfunctioning. "Should we call the power company?"

Daniel pulled out his phone, but the screen was black. He pressed the power button—nothing. "That's weird. Phone's dead, too." He tried his backup battery bank, but it remained stubbornly lifeless.

Ryan thundered down the stairs, nearly colliding with the antique side table they'd bought at that auction in Boston. "Mom! My PlayStation turned off in the middle of—" He stopped, seeing their faces. At seven, he was already learning to read the room.

"Let's make it an adventure," Jessica said brightly, her real estate agent's ability to spin any situation coming in handy. "We can have dinner by candlelight."

Daniel nodded absently, trying his laptop. Dead. His iPad. Dead. Everything electronic had simply… stopped. The unease in his stomach grew. He'd been on the phone with his father when the call cut out—something about Old Man Jenkins and solar storms. He'd been distracted, focused on a client's portfolio concerns, and now he couldn't remember the details.

By 8:45, they'd managed to salvage a decent dinner. Jessica had rescued the soon to be thawing salmon from their Sub-Zero freezer, cooking it on their gas range while the children arranged battery-operated candles from their emergency kit around the formal dining room.

"When will the power come back?" Lily asked around a mouthful of fish.

Before Daniel could answer, Ryan pointed to the window. "Look at the sky!"

Through their floor-to-ceiling windows, designed to showcase their professionally landscaped yard, they could see ribbons of light beginning to dance across the darkening sky. Green and purple waves shimmered impossibly, like something from a nature documentary about Alaska.

"Aurora," Daniel whispered. "This far south?"

A sharp knock at their front door made Jessica jump, her fork clattering against fine china.

Through the decorative glass panels, they could see Austin Williams from down the street—a fellow financial advisor they often golfed with at the country club. His usual polished appearance was slightly disheveled.

"Thompson." Marcus's voice was tight as Daniel opened the door. "You getting anything on your devices? The trading systems went down right before the power cut. Nothing's working. Nothing."

Daniel shook his head. "Everything's dead. Even battery packs won't work."

More neighbors were emerging now, drawn by the darkness and the strange lights in the sky. Their carefully manicured lawns and architect-designed homes felt suddenly fragile under the aurora's alien glow.

"My father tried to warn me," Daniel said quietly. "Called right before everything went down. Something about solar storms."

Jessica appeared beside him, her voice low. "Should we be worried?"

Daniel thought about his father's farm, about the skills his brothers had that he'd left behind for the financial world. "Maybe," he admitted. "But let's not scare the kids tonight."

As if on cue, Lily's voice carried from the dining room: "Daddy! The ice cream's going to melt!"

Daniel felt a genuine smile tug at his lips. "Well then," he announced, closing the front door. "I guess we better eat it."

Jessica caught his mood. "And you know what goes perfectly with ice cream for dinner?" She paused dramatically as both children leaned forward. "Family game night. I think it's finally time to break out that Monopoly set Aunt Emily gave you for Christmas."

"I want to be the racecar!" Ryan called, already rushing toward the game cabinet.

"No fair! You're always the racecar!" Lily protested, running after him.

They spent the next hour by candlelight, eating rapidly softening ice cream straight from the containers and playing board games. The aurora cast shifting colors through the windows, but inside their home, the warm glow of battery-operated candles and children's laughter kept the strangeness at bay.

When the kids finally went to bed—after negotiating for "just one more round" three times—Daniel and Jessica stood in the darkness of their kitchen. Their eyes met, a wordless exchange that contained both their fears about what was coming and their shared determination to protect their children from it. Jessica's hand found his, squeezing gently: a gesture that meant both *I'm scared* and *we'll figure this out* all at once.

"I'll take care of the clean up," Jessica said softly, gathering the sticky ice cream containers and spoons and wiping up sticky spots, while Daniel headed for the garage.

The '72 Ford pickup sat in the far bay, his weekend project for months now—something his financial sector colleagues had teased him about. Who restored old trucks in Lynnfield? But as he pulled the manual release for the garage door, he found himself grateful for its simple mechanics.

The aurora's strange light filtered through the garage windows, casting otherworldly shadows across the truck's half-restored form. No electronic fuel injection. No computer-controlled engine management. Just simple mechanics and engineering, the kind his father had taught him before he'd chosen suits and trading floors over the family farm.

His father's words from their cut-off phone call echoed in his mind. Something about Old Man Jenkins ranting about solar storms, about the grid failing. At the time, he'd been distracted by a client's portfolio concerns. Now…

Through the window, he could see other houses in their subdivision—dark shapes against the illuminated sky. Some had candles flickering in windows. Others were completely dark. The neighborhood felt different now, more fragile. All their carefully curated lives, their investment portfolios, their private school plans—none of it meant anything if the world had really changed.

The truck needed work before it would run. Maybe a day, maybe less if he focused. But it would run. And then…

Daniel closed the hood quietly, his decision already forming. The aurora pulsed overhead, painting his garage in impossible colors, as he stood there thinking about farms and fathers and the things that really mattered when the world stopped making sense.

Daniel returned from the garage to find Jessica at the gas stove, the familiar hiss of their Italian coffee maker a strange comfort in the silent house. The battery-powered lantern cast dramatic shadows across the kitchen—all the stainless steel and marble that had seemed so important when they'd renovated last spring now felt superfluous.

"At least we can still make coffee," Jessica said, trying for lightness but not quite hitting the mark. She'd changed into her silk pajamas, an absurd bit of normalcy in their now-altered world.

Daniel settled at their kitchen island, watching the aurora's light dance across the professional-grade appliances. "We need to talk about leaving."

"Leaving?" Jessica's hand tightened around her coffee cup. "Daniel, this is temporary. The power company—"

"Will do what?" Daniel's voice was soft but firm. "Drive their electric trucks? Use their computerized systems? Call for supplies on dead phones?" He gestured toward their dark refrigerator. "That's eight thousand dollars of SubZero that's now just an oversized paperweight."

"So we'll lose some food. Insurance will—"

"Insurance?" Daniel cut her off, then caught himself, lowering his voice to avoid waking the kids. "Jess, think about it. Really think. No computers. No phones. No electronic banking. No credit cards. How long before people realize that all their money, all their assets, are just numbers in dead computers?"

Jessica sank onto the bar stool beside him, her face pale in the lantern light. "You're talking about…"

"Anarchy," Daniel finished. "Maybe not today. Maybe not tomorrow. But soon." He took a sip of coffee, buying time to organize his thoughts. "Look around this neighborhood. Look what we have. How long before people from Revere, from Lynn, realize that Lynnfield is full of unprotected homes with enough food and supplies to feed families for months?"

"We have the security system—"

"Which is dead," Daniel said gently. "Along with every other protection we thought we had." He reached for her hand. "My father's farm—"

"The farm?" Jessica pulled away, standing abruptly. "You want us to leave our home, our life, everything we've built to go live on a farm in Maine?" Her voice cracked slightly. "What about the children? Their schools, their friends—"

"Their lives," Daniel finished. "Because that's what we're talking about now. Not education plans or play dates or soccer practice. Survival."

Jessica paced the kitchen, her silk pajamas catching the aurora's light. "This is insane. We have a life here. Connections. Status. You're talking about throwing it all away because of one power outage—"

"This isn't a power outage," Daniel said, his voice taking on an edge. "This is something else. Something worse. My father tried to warn me, but I was too busy with the fucking Morgan account to listen." He ran a hand through his hair. "The simple fact is, this house, this neighborhood—it's not sustainable. We can't protect it."

"So we just run?" Jessica's voice rose. "Hide out on a farm like… like…"

"Like survivors?" Daniel stood, moving to the window. In the distance, he could see something burning—the orange glow of fire against the aurora-lit sky. "Look out there. Really look. No street lights. No police cars patrolling. No cameras watching. Just darkness and a lot of desperate people about to realize that all the rules have changed."

Jessica joined him at the window, her anger deflating slightly. "I see our home. Our neighborhood. Our life."

"I see targets," Daniel said quietly. "Rich targets with no real defenses. How many guns in Lynnfield, Jess? How many people here know how to really fight, to really survive? We've got Range Rovers and security systems and country club memberships. What good is any of that now? Listen, if the lights come back, so will we, but I think this is the best choice. If we wait, it might be too late."

They stood in silence, watching the distant fire grow.

"The farm has food," Daniel continued softly. "Real food, not just whatever's in our pantry. It has water that doesn't depend on electric pumps. It has people who know how to live without computers and credit cards. Most importantly, it has my family."

Jessica's hand found his, trembling slightly. "I'm scared," she whispered.

"I know." He pulled her close. "I'm terrified. But not as terrified as I am of staying here, watching our neighborhood turn into a war zone while we try to protect our children with nothing but good intentions and dead appliances."

The coffee had grown cold, forgotten on the kitchen island. The aurora's light seemed to mock their carefully curated life— the art pieces that had seemed so important, the smart home features now rendered stupid, the status symbols transformed into liabilities.

"When?" Jessica finally asked, her voice small.

"Soon. As soon as I can get the truck running." He felt her tense. "Not the Mercedes. The old Ford. The one you hate."

A quiet laugh escaped her. "I don't hate it now."

They stood together, watching the fire in the distance grow brighter. Somewhere in the darkness, a window shattered—the sound sharp and final in the unnaturally quiet night. Jessica flinched.

"The kids," she whispered. "How do we explain…"

"We tell them it's an adventure," Daniel said, though his throat tightened at the thought. "We tell them we're going to visit Grandpa's farm for a while. We don't tell them that 'a while' might be forever."

Jessica turned into his chest, her tears dampening his shirt. "I don't know how to live on a farm."

"We'll learn." He stroked her hair, watching another fire bloom in the distance. "We'll learn because we have to."

They stood there until the coffee was completely cold, holding each other in their dark kitchen, surrounded by all the useless trappings of their former life. Eventually, they made their way upstairs, both knowing sleep would be impossible but needing to try anyway.

As they passed the children's rooms, Jessica paused. "Promise me something?"

"Anything."

"Promise me we're not just trading one kind of helplessness for another."

Daniel thought about his father's hands, strong and sure on the farm equipment. Thought about the skills he'd left behind in his rush to conquer the financial world. "We're trading paper wealth for real wealth," he said finally. "Food. Water. Family. Community. The things that matter when everything else falls apart."

In their bedroom, the aurora painted strange patterns on their expensive sheets. Neither of them mentioned the growing number of fires on the horizon, or the increasing frequency of breaking glass in the distance.

Maddie

Three Hours Post CME—Boston, Massachusetts

THE WORLD HAD GONE SILENT. NOT JUST QUIET, absolutely, oppressively silent. No hum of electricity, no distant sounds of air conditioning, no background buzz of technology that had always been there, unnoticed until it vanished completely.

Maddie's feet ached. Her designer sandals—perfect for a day tour of Harvard—were now instruments of torture as they trudged through the increasingly dark streets of Boston. The July heat hadn't broken, instead becoming a suffocating blanket that made every breath feel thick, heavy with impending darkness.

"We should go back to the train station," Grace chirped, her voice bizarrely cheerful. "It's got big windows. Lots of space. And those guys were cute. Maybe we could, like, talk to them?"

Hannah's hand shot out, gripping Grace's arm. "Those guys were sizing us up like we were potential targets. Not potential dates."

Grace pulled away, her strawberry-blonde ponytail swinging. "You're being dramatic. Things will be fine tomorrow. Probably just a big power outage. My dad says these things happen all the time." She pulled out her dead phone, tapping it uselessly. "I bet if we just find a charger—"

"The entire electrical grid is down," Maddie said, her voice a razor's edge of controlled panic. "This isn't a local outage. This is… something else."

The street was a wasteland of abandoned cars. Some doors hung open, as if people had simply abandoned them mid-journey. No traffic lights worked. No street lights flickered. The only illumination came from the dying summer sunlight, casting long, menacing shadows that seemed to move with a life of their own.

Grace continued her denial. "My internship starts next week. I can't miss that. I've been planning this all summer." She laughed, a high, brittle sound that didn't match the apocalyptic landscape around them. "Someone will fix this. They always do."

Maddie stopped walking. Her small town pragmatism—inherited from generations of coastal Maine families who knew how to survive—was battling her rising fear. "We need shelter. Real shelter. Not an open train station where anyone can walk in."

Hannah's eyes constantly moved, scanning their surroundings. "Somewhere with few entry points. Somewhere we can make secure."

"Oh my God, you guys are being so dramatic," Grace whined. "I'm sure the power company is already—"

"The power company isn't coming," Hannah snapped. The first real crack in her composure showed—a tremor in her voice that betrayed the terror underneath her practical exterior.

The smell of hot asphalt mixed with something else—fear.

A primal, animal scent that spoke of survival and impending danger. Sweat traced lines down Maddie's back. Her designer summer top was now a liability—thin, offering no protection.

Grace pulled out her dead phone again. Tap. Tap. Tap. A rhythmic denial of reality.

"We need to move," Maddie said. "Now. Before it gets completely dark."

The first fire erupted two blocks from the train station—a violent bloom of orange and red against the darkening sky. The smell hit them first: burning plastic, scorched wood, something acrid and chemical that made Maddie's eyes water.

A scream echoed between the buildings. Then another.

Grace's whimpering began low, then crescendoed. "I want to go home," she said, her voice rising hysterically. "I want my mother. This isn't happening. This can't be happening."

Hannah grabbed her arm, jerking her forward. "Keep moving. Stay quiet."

Another fire. Then another. The city was burning in disconnected patches, like fevered patches on dying skin. No sirens. No fire trucks. Nothing but the crackle of flames and distant, terrified human sounds.

Grace's ill fitting found sandals—now covered in street grime—clicked against the pavement. Each step a protest. "My phone won't work. My laptop won't work. How am I supposed to—" Her voice broke.

Maddie's leadership instinct battled her own rising terror. "We need to find shelter. Something we can lock. Something defensible."

The auroras began overhead—not the soft, beautiful light of scientific documentaries, but a violent, churning display.

Greens and purples twisted like living things, casting an alien light over the burning city. The electromagnetic display was beautiful and terrifying, painting everything in unnatural colors.

Grace began to full-on sob. "I'm scared. I'm so scared."

Maddie, Hannah, and Grace pressed themselves against the corner of a brick building, peering cautiously around the edge at the main street.

The sudden explosion of shattering glass made Grace jump. A storefront window disintegrated, spray-painted shards cascading onto the sidewalk.

"Oh my—" Grace started to scream.

Maddie's hand clamped down hard over her mouth, her fingers pressing so tightly Grace's muffled cry was barely a whisper. Hannah's arm wrapped around Grace's waist, physically dragging her into the narrow alley.

They crouched behind a rusted dumpster, the smell of rotting garbage and hot metal mixing with the distant smell of burning.

Footsteps. Voices.

"I know I heard something," a gravelly male voice said.

A woman's laugh cut through the darkness—high-pitched, almost maniacal. "Look at this!" she cackled. "The good stuff's in here!"

More footsteps. The sound of something heavy being dragged.

Grace trembled, tears streaming silently down her cheeks. Maddie's hand remained firmly over her mouth, her eyes locked on the mouth of the alley, watching. Waiting.

The voices moved closer. Then—miraculously—began to recede.

The moment Maddie released her grip, Grace erupted. "You hurt me! You were choking me! That was—"

Hannah's hand shot out, slapping Grace hard across the face. The sound echoed in the narrow alley.

Silence.

Grace stared, shocked. Her hand slowly came up to touch her reddened cheek. For the first time since the CME hit, she was utterly silent. Truly scared. Something inside her suddenly seemed lost, and Maddie wrapped an arm around her.

They emerged from the alley cautiously, the alien aurora light casting strange shadows. Returning to where the window had been shattered they paused and looked through the broken storefront window of the pawn shop, they spotted an elderly man curled on the floor, whimpering. Blood trickled from a cut on his temple.

"Oh my God," Hannah whispered. Her medical training kicked in instantly. "We can't just leave him."

They entered carefully, Hannah approaching first. "Sir? Sir, we're not going to hurt you."

The old man flinched, trying to scramble backward. His fear was palpable—raw and animal.

"I'm a medical student," Hannah said softly. "Let me help you."

Something in her tone—professional, calm—seemed to break through his terror.

The store smelled of copper and fear—old blood mixing with the metallic scent of broken glass and spilled merchandise. Shelves lay toppled, a lifetime of carefully ordered inventory now scattered across the floor. A cash register lay on its side, drawer open and empty, its mechanical innards exposed like a wounded animal.

The old man cowered near a display case, his trembling hands raised defensively. Deep purple bruising bloomed across his cheekbone, and a jagged cut above his eye wept a thin line of blood. His terrified eyes darted between the three young women, seeing threats where only help existed.

"Please," he whispered, his voice breaking. "Please don't hurt me."

Hannah moved slowly, her medical training evident in every careful step. "Sir, we're not going to harm you. I can help clean your wound."

Grace stood back, uncharacteristically quiet. The violence, the fear—it was finally sinking in. This wasn't a temporary inconvenience. This was real.

Maddie scanned the destroyed storefront, her protective instincts flaring. "We need to get him somewhere safe," she murmured to Hannah.

The old man's trembling increased. "Martha," he called out weakly. "Martha, help me."

An elderly woman appeared from a doorway in the back, her worried face a map of concern and fear. She took in the scene—three young women, her injured husband, the destroyed store—with surprising calm.

"Come," she said simply. "Upstairs. Now."

The wooden stairs creaked under their weight, each step a potential betrayal of their presence. Martha moved ahead, her movements deliberate, eyes constantly scanning back toward her husband and their unexpected guests.

Their apartment was a time capsule—vintage furniture, photographs yellowed with age, doilies on side tables. But the windows told a different story. The auroras outside cast everything in an unnatural green-purple light, transforming the mundane into something alien and threatening.

Hannah kneeled beside the old man, her medical bag—miraculously still with her from the Harvard tour—open beside her. "This might sting," she warned, cleaning the wound with an antiseptic wipe.

The old man—Harold, Martha called him—winced but didn't pull away. His eyes never left the windows, watching the strange lights dance across the broken cityscape.

"They took everything," Harold murmured. "Decades of work. Gone in moments."

Martha disappeared into the kitchen, returning with a battered tin of crackers and some preserved meat. "You should eat," she commanded the girls, her voice brooking no argument.

Grace, still shell-shocked, accepted the food mechanically. Maddie's eyes constantly moved—checking the stairs, the windows, scanning for potential threats.

"We need to get back to Maine," Maddie said quietly. "We have no other option."

Hannah nearly sobbing as she spoke said, "We don't even know where we are."

Martha's weathered hand trembled as she placed a plate of crackers and the preserved meat on the table. Her eyes, clouded with cataracts but still sharp with intelligence, swept over the three young women.

"You're not going anywhere tonight," she said firmly. It wasn't a suggestion, but a declaration. "this is East Boston. Not a place for young ladies to go wandering at night alone."

Harold winced as Hannah continued cleaning his wound.

The bruises on his face told a story of violence that made Grace—who had been silent since the slap—look away, her earlier bravado completely stripped away.

"We have to get home," Maddie protested, but her voice lacked its earlier conviction.

Martha's laugh was brittle, painful. "Home?" She gestured to the window, where the aurora painted the broken city in impossible colors. "Look out there. There is no 'home' right now. Not for anyone."

She moved slowly, each step careful, to a small pantry. "I've lived through hard times," Martha said. "World War II. The Cuban Missile Crisis. This—" she swept her hand toward the window, "—this is different."

Harold reached out, taking his wife's hand. The gesture was so tender, so filled with decades of shared understanding, that it made the girls fall silent.

"You'll stay," Martha said. "We have a spare room. You'll be safe here."

The room remained tense, but Martha's maternal presence began to soften the edges of their fear. Maddie positioned herself near the window, her body a coiled spring of alertness. From this vantage point, she could watch the street below—a landscape of broken glass, abandoned cars, and the occasional distant flicker of unexplained fires.

"Sit," Martha instructed, her voice leaving no room for argument. Each movement was a testament to her age—shoulders slightly hunched, steps measured and careful. Years of life etched into every gesture.

Hannah stood immediately. "Let me help you," she offered, moving toward the kitchen.

Martha's kitchen was a shrine to another era. Copper pots hung from hooks that looked older than the woman herself. An old gas stove dominated one wall, its surface worn smooth by decades of use. Jars of preserved vegetables lined shelves. Not at all what the girls would expect from the high tech areas they were familiar with.

"Tea," Martha murmured. "And something to eat. You can't travel on an empty stomach."

Harold remained seated, Hannah's careful medical attention having calmed his earlier terror. The bruises on his face grew in both size and color and he winced when she checked the bandage.

Maddie's mind wandered to her home and her family while watching the aurora continue its otherworldly dance outside, casting strange shadows through the kitchen window. Green and purple light transformed the most mundane objects into something alien and beautiful.

"We wanted to find shelter," Grace hesitantly said, snapping Maddie's attention from the window.

"Oh my God, Grace. I'm so sorry about--! I only wanted to…"

"I know." Grace said, meekly. "I didn't know."

Maddie hurried to her and wrapped her arms around her, sobbing. The day's events finally crashed in her mind. She had to face the reality that this was real.

Grace pressed her back and said, "We did want to find shelter, right?"

"Yes, of course," Maddie said, standing and wiping her running nose with her hand. "Thank you, Martha. I can't tell you how much this helps us."

The old woman smiled, setting a large pot of very tasty smelling stew on the table.

James

Ten Minutes Post CME—Cornish, Maine

THE SILENCE WAS DEAFENING.

James Thompson stood in his kitchen, his calloused hand still gripping the edge of the counter where he'd braced himself when everything electronic had died. The house felt wrong— fundamentally wrong—in a way he couldn't quite articulate. The perpetual hum of modern life had vanished, replaced by an emptiness that made his skin crawl.

"James?" Sarah's voice wavered slightly as she stared at the dead microwave. "I'm sure the power company will have this fixed soon. Remember that big outage in '98?"

He didn't respond immediately, instead watching Michael through the window. His son-in-law had immediately moved to the barn, every movement deliberate. Emily followed close behind him, her steps quick and anxious.

"Dad?" Matthew's voice cracked. He was still holding his now-useless phone, jabbing at it frantically. "This doesn't make sense. The battery was at ninety percent. How can everything just… die?"

Elena let out a small whimper from the living room couch, her hands protectively cradling her pregnant belly. "The baby… I can't feel the baby moving." Panic edged into her voice.

"Matthew? Matthew, I need help."

James watched his youngest son's face drain of color. The transformation from confident tech professional to terrified expectant father happened in an instant. "I'll call Dr. Stevens—" Matthew started, then stared at his dead phone in horror. "I can't… I can't call anyone."

"Sit down, Elena," Sarah said, her teacher's instincts kicking in despite her own fear. "The baby's fine. You're just having a panic attack. Deep breaths."

The July heat pressed against the windows, somehow more oppressive now without the gentle whir of air conditioning. A bead of sweat traced down James's neck as he mentally cataloged everything that had just changed. The well pump—electric. The refrigerator—dead. The chest freezer in the basement, full of last season's meat. All their modern communications were gone.

The distant sound of something exploding made Elena jump. Matthew rushed to the window. "Oh God," he whispered. "The transformers. Look at the power lines."

James didn't need to look. He could smell it—the acrid scent of electrical fires, carrying on the hot summer breeze. More explosions followed, a cascading series of pops and bangs that marked the death of the power grid.

Michael burst through the door, Emily close behind him. His face was set in hard lines, the training evident in his bearing. "James," he said without preamble, "we need to talk. Now."

"The baby," Elena sobbed. "Please, someone needs to check on the baby. I can't… I can't feel…"

"Emily," James said quietly, "get Elena upstairs to lie down. Sarah, go with them." His voice was steady, betraying none of the ice-cold fear that had settled in his stomach. "Matthew, help your girlfriend up the stairs."

"But my phone," Matthew protested weakly. "There has to be a way to—"

"Matthew." James's tone left no room for argument. "Your girlfriend needs you. Now."

As the women helped Elena upstairs, her soft sobs echoing through the suddenly too-quiet house, James turned to Michael. His son-in-law's expression confirmed every dark thought forming in James's mind.

"CME," Michael said flatly. "Coronal Mass Ejection. Jenkins was right."

"Jesus," James muttered. "You really think—"

"Everything's dead, James. Everything. This isn't a normal power outage." Michael moved to the window, his posture tense. "I did training exercises for this scenario. Never thought I'd actually see it."

The sound of Matthew's panicked voice drifted down from upstairs, followed by Elena's continued crying. Sarah's soothing tones tried to maintain calm, but there was an edge of hysteria building.

"How bad?" James asked simply.

Michael's laugh was hollow. "Bad. If it's strong enough to fry electronics like this? We're looking at a complete infrastructure collapse. No power grid. No communications. No transportation systems. Modern medicine goes back two hundred years overnight."

The implications hit James like a physical blow. Elena's pregnancy. The community's dependence on electricity. The coming harvest. Winter storage. His hands clenched involuntarily.

"The town will need organization," Michael continued. "Leadership. You're on the council. People trust you."

A crash from upstairs made them both turn. Matthew's voice rose in pitch. "What do you mean you can't find a heartbeat? You have to try harder!"

James closed his eyes briefly. "The doppler monitor. It's electronic."

"Everything's electronic," Michael confirmed grimly. "We need to—"

The sound of running feet on the stairs cut him off. Matthew appeared, his face wild with fear. "The monitor's not working. Nothing's working. Elena's crying. Mom's trying to calm her down but… Dad, what do we do?"

James looked at his son—really looked at him. Matthew, with his tech startup dreams and his modern life, suddenly seemed very young and very lost. The carefully constructed world of computers and smartphones and instant communication had crumbled in minutes, leaving him unmoored.

"First," James said carefully, "you go back upstairs and be with your girlfriend. She needs you calm. Can you do that?"

Matthew's breath came in short gasps. "But the baby… if we can't monitor… if we can't reach the doctor…"

"Matthew." James gripped his son's shoulders. "Your job right now is to be strong for Elena. Everything else comes after that. Understand?"

A strangled sob escaped Matthew's throat. For a moment, James saw the little boy who used to run to him with scraped knees and broken toys, expecting his father to fix everything.

But this couldn't be fixed with a band-aid or some superglue.

"I can't," Matthew whispered. "Dad, I can't do this. All my savings… our accounts… the new house down payment… it's all digital. Everything we planned…"

Michael stepped forward. "One problem at a time, Matt. Right now, Elena needs you. Go. We'll figure out the rest."

As Matthew stumbled back upstairs, James moved to the kitchen window. The view was deceptively normal—fields stretching toward the horizon, the barn standing solid and eternal, the summer sky a brilliant blue. But the silence felt like a physical presence, pressing against his ears.

"We need to inventory everything," Michael said quietly. "Food. Water. Medical supplies. Anything that doesn't require power. The chest freezer in the basement—"

"Will start thawing soon," James finished. "All that meat…"

"We can smoke some of it. Like your grandfather used to do." Michael's mind was clearly racing. "The root cellar will help. But we need to act fast."

More sobs from upstairs. Emily's voice now, trying to be practical: "Elena, sweetie, try to feel for movement. Put your hand right here…"

Sarah appeared at the bottom of the stairs, her face pale. "James? Elena's really struggling. The baby… we can't find the heartbeat with the monitor, and she's convinced something's wrong. Matthew's not helping. He's… he's not handling this well."

The weight of responsibility settled across James's shoulders like a physical burden. He thought of Jenkins' warnings, all those conversations about preparation and infrastructure collapse. He'd listened politely, considering the old man slightly paranoid. Now…

"Michael," he said quietly, "check the barn. Make sure the manual equipment is accessible. Then we need to inventory everything. Sarah, find Emily's old stethoscope from her nursing days. Maybe we can hear the baby's heartbeat the old-fashioned way."

"James," Sarah's voice cracked slightly. "What's really happening?"

He looked at his wife of thirty-five years, seeing the fear she was trying to hide. The same fear he was burying beneath layers of practical consideration. "I don't know," he admitted. "But whatever it is, we need to be ready."

Another distant explosion made the windows rattle slightly. The smell of electrical fires was stronger now, carried on the hot summer breeze. Upstairs, Elena's sobs had quieted to hiccupping breaths, punctuated by Matthew's attempts at comfort that sounded more like desperation.

Michael headed for the barn, his movements precise and controlled. Sarah went to search for the stethoscope, her hands shaking slightly. And James… James stood in his kitchen, listening to the unnatural silence, feeling the weight of what was coming settle into his bones.

The world they'd known was ending. Not with a bang or a whimper, but with a silence that felt like a scream.

Minutes stretched like hours. James forced himself to move methodically, checking each room downstairs. The refrigerator would hold its cold for a while if they kept it closed. The chest freezer in the basement was better insulated, but eventually… He pushed the thought aside. One problem at a time.

Sarah's footsteps echoed as she rummaged through closets upstairs, searching for Emily's old medical equipment. Elena's crying had subsided into occasional whimpers, but Matthew's voice still carried an edge of hysteria as he attempted reassurance.

"Found it!" Sarah's voice rang out, followed by quick footsteps. Emily appeared at the top of the stairs, taking the old stethoscope from her mother's trembling hands. Her face was set in determined lines, channeling her previous nursing training.

"Elena, honey," Emily called out, "we're going to do this the old-fashioned way, okay?"

James watched Michael through the window as his son-in-law methodically checked the barn's manual tools. The military precision of his movements was somehow reassuring—at least someone knew how to operate in a crisis.

A sound from the basement made James turn. Matthew stood at the bottom of the stairs, his face ashen. "The servers," he whispered. "My backup drives. Everything's fried. Years of work, all my client data…" His hands shook as he ran them through his hair. "Oh God, the banking systems. Our savings…"

"Matthew." James kept his voice steady. "Your wife needs you upstairs."

"You don't understand!" Matthew's voice rose sharply. "Everything's gone! My whole career—our future—it's all digital! All of it! The down payment for the house, Elena's maternity leave fund…" He slammed his fist against the wall, the sharp crack making Sarah jump. "I was supposed to provide for them!"

"And you will," James said firmly, though his own mind

was racing through implications. How many others would be realizing this same thing? How many lives were built entirely on digital foundations that had just crumbled?

The sound of a vehicle approaching made them all freeze. Through the window, James saw Old Man Jenkins's truck sputtering down the drive—one of the few vehicles still running, probably because of its age and simple mechanics.

Michael jogged in from the barn. "Pre-1980s vehicles," he said grimly through the now open window as he hurried past. "No computer systems. They're still working. For now, at least, until we run out of gas."

Jenkins practically fell out of his truck, his weathered face wild with a mixture of vindication and terror. "Thompson! The radio operators—my contacts—they're all going dark. One after another. It's happening everywhere!"

Upstairs, a cry of relief cut through the tension. "I found it!" Emily called out. "Elena, listen—that's your baby's heartbeat. Strong and steady!"

For a moment, joy pierced the growing darkness. Matthew's face transformed, tears streaming down his cheeks as he bolted upstairs. Sarah pressed her hand to her mouth, a sob of relief escaping.

But Jenkins wasn't finished. "The military channels," he continued, his voice shaking. "Before they went dark… Thompson, this isn't just us. It's everywhere. The whole grid, the whole country…" He grabbed James's arm. "We need to tell people. Need to organize. While there's still time."

"Time for what?" Sarah asked, her voice small.

Michael answered before Jenkins could in clipped tones. "Before panic sets in. Before people realize their money is gone, their cars won't start, their phones won't work. Before the food in their freezers starts to rot."

Through the window, James could see a few people were walking, looking dazed and confused in the summer heat and headed toward downtown.

"The hospital," Emily said suddenly, appearing at the top of the stairs. "Their backup generators…"

"Won't last forever," Michael finished. "A few days at most, if they're lucky."

Elena's voice drifted down, stronger now that she'd heard her baby's heartbeat. "But what about when it's time? What about when the baby comes?"

The question hung in the air, heavy with implications. James looked at his family—Sarah's trembling hands, Matthew's tear-streaked face as he helped Elena down the stairs, Emily's determined expression, Michael's tactical assessment of their situation. All of them expecting him to have answers he wasn't sure he could offer, when something caught his eye.

The kids sat in the main room by the light of the now open window, playing a game of dinosaurs on the carpet. Oblivious to anything other than the fact that the power went out. James' expression changed as worry for them crept into his face, and he turned away to look at the road out front.

Beyond the glass and reflections of questions within, the setting July sun beat down on a world that had fundamentally changed in less than an hour. More exploding transformers, more people walking, more confusion spreading. Soon, James knew, confusion would turn to fear. Fear would turn to panic. And panic…

Maddie

That Night—Boston, Massachusetts

NONE OF THEM COULD SLEEP, NOT REALLY. THE apartment above the store had become their fortress, but the walls felt paper-thin against the chaos erupting across Boston. Maddie sat by the window, mesmerized by the impossible light show dancing across the sky. The aurora rippled like a living thing—violent greens and purples painting the burning city in alien hues.

"It's beautiful," Hannah whispered, joining her at the window. "In a terrifying sort of way."

A woman's scream cut through the night, followed by the sound of breaking glass. Grace, huddled in the corner with her useless phone still clutched in her hands, let out a quiet sob.

"Make it stop," Grace whimpered. "Please, just make it stop."

Martha moved like a ghost through the apartment, checking windows, adjusting the blackout curtains she'd insisted on hanging. The smell of smoke grew stronger as the night deepened, and occasional explosions lit up the sky—transformers blowing, Harold had explained, or maybe gas lines.

"In the war," Martha said softly, pausing near their

window, "we had air raids. But at least then we knew who the enemy was." She gestured to the aurora-lit chaos outside. "This? This is humanity turning on itself."

A burst of gunfire echoed between the buildings—sharp cracks that made them all flinch. It sounded closer than the last one. Grace's whimpering increased in pitch.

"Shh," Hannah moved to comfort her, but Grace jerked away.

"Don't touch me! This isn't real. This can't be real!" Her voice rose dangerously.

Maddie crossed the room quickly, clamping a hand over Grace's mouth. "We have to stay quiet," she hissed. "Sound carries."

Through the window, the aurora cast everything in an eerie glow. A car was burning two blocks away, the flames reaching up toward the otherworldly lights. The smoke made Maddie's eyes water, or maybe those were tears she was refusing to acknowledge.

"Three young men tried to break into the Millers' place," Harold reported, returning from checking the back stairs. His bruised face looked ghostly in the strange light. "Tom Miller shot one of them."

The information hung in the air like the smoke—heavy, suffocating. These were their neighbors. Their community. Less than twenty-four hours without power, and everything was falling apart.

More screaming. More gunshots. The sound of breaking glass had become almost constant, a terrible background music to their nightmare. The aurora pulsed overhead, as if responding to the chaos below.

Grace started humming to herself—a high, keening sound that made the hair on Maddie's neck stand up. Hannah caught Maddie's eye, and they shared a look of growing concern.

"Try to rest," Martha advised, though she made no move toward her own bed. "Tomorrow will be harder than today."

Maddie couldn't imagine anything harder than this—sitting in the dark, watching civilization crumble under an impossible sky. But as another explosion rocked the night and Grace's humming grew louder, she realized tomorrow would bring its own horrors.

The aurora continued its deadly, beautiful dance, casting strange shadows across their faces as they waited for a dawn none of them were sure would come.

Maddie woke to the acrid taste of smoke coating her tongue. Her muscles ached from sleeping on the hard floor, and the early morning light filtering through the windows carried an eerie orange tint from the still-burning fires across Boston. The aurora continued its ghostly dance overhead, casting unnatural shadows across the room.

Grace's whimpers had become a constant backdrop, like the distant gunshots that punctuated the morning air. "I can't— I can't do this anymore," she mumbled, rocking slightly. "My phone's still dead. This isn't happening."

"Shh," Hannah whispered, her gentle but firm tone trying to calm her. "We need to stay quiet, Grace. Sound carries."

Martha appeared from the kitchen, moving with surprising stealth for her age. The smell of something herbal—tea, maybe—mingled with the omnipresent smoke. "Eat," she commanded, setting down a plate of preserved meat and hard biscuits. "You'll need your strength."

Another explosion echoed in the distance, making Grace jump. Maddie's hand instinctively reached for her friend, but Hannah got there first, steadying her.

"We can't leave you here," Hannah insisted to Martha, her voice tight with concern. "The city's falling apart. Come with us."

Harold emerged from the back room, his bruised face a testament to yesterday's violence. "This is our home," he said simply. "We've lived here fifty years. We'll die here if need be."

Martha began pulling items from various hiding spots around the apartment. "The world's changed," she said, her movements purposeful. "You'll need proper gear." She held up a pair of sturdy walking shoes. "These should fit you better than those fancy things you're wearing, dear."

Maddie took the shoes, noting how the leather felt worn but solid. Another burst of gunfire, closer this time, made them all flinch. The smell of smoke seemed to intensify, burning her nostrils.

"But my internship," Grace started again, her voice rising hysterically. "I can't just—"

"Grace," Maddie cut her off, perhaps too sharply. "There are no internships anymore. We need to focus on getting home."

Harold gestured for them to follow him downstairs, each creaking step making Maddie wince. The store below still showed signs of yesterday's violence—broken glass crunching under their feet, merchandise scattered across the floor.

"My brother will kill me if I don't make it home," Hannah muttered, adjusting the wool blanket and sheets Martha had given her to carry. "He always said Boston would be a death trap in a crisis."

The back room smelled different from upstairs—musty, with undertones of oil and rubber. Harold moved aside some boxes, revealing three bicycles. "They're not much," he said, "but they'll get you moving faster than walking."

Grace stared at the bikes, clutching her newly assigned supplies—food tin, utensils, and rope—to her chest like a shield. "I haven't ridden since I was twelve," she whispered, terror evident in her voice.

Another explosion rocked the building, closer than any before. Dust filtered down from the ceiling, and somewhere in the distance, someone screamed.

"It's like riding a bike," Maddie said, attempting humor that fell flat in the smoke-filled air. She adjusted the small tent Martha had given her to carry, testing its weight. "You never forget."

The sound of breaking glass from somewhere nearby made them all freeze. Martha's hand tightened on Harold's arm.

"You need to go," Martha urged, her voice barely above a whisper. "Now. Take the back alley. Stay off the main streets."

Martha hugged each girl in turn, her thin arms surprisingly strong. When she reached Grace, she held on a bit longer, as if trying to pour strength into the trembling young woman. "Remember what I told you about boiling water," she said, her voice thick with emotion. "Every time. Even if you think it's clean."

A woman's scream pierced the morning air, followed by the sound of shattering glass. Grace jumped, but Martha held her steady.

"Please," Hannah tried one last time, her voice cracking

with concern. "You're not safe here. The city's dying. Come with us."

Harold took Martha's hand, their weathered fingers intertwining with the familiarity of decades. "We've been in this building since 1983," he said softly. "Helped birth some of our neighbors' children right here in this store. Mrs. Rodriguez upstairs—she's diabetic. Who'll help her measure her insulin? And the Chen family next door, their youngest is deaf. They rely on us to interpret the news."

"But—" Maddie started, but Martha cut her off with a gentle touch to her cheek.

"Some people run," she said, her clouded eyes sharp with wisdom. "Some people stand. We're standers, dear. Always have been."

Another explosion rocked the building. This time, Grace didn't jump—she was too busy crying.

"You girls," Martha's voice wavered for the first time, "you remind me so much of my daughters at your age. They're gone now—cancer took them both years ago. But seeing you…" She pulled handkerchiefs from her pocket, pressing one into each of their hands. "I've been saving these. They were meant for my granddaughters."

The handkerchiefs were delicate, hand-embroidered with tiny flowers. Maddie's vision blurred as she ran her fingers over the stitching.

"Harold," Martha called over her shoulder, never taking her eyes off the girls, "the package."

Harold disappeared into the back room, returning with a small paper-wrapped bundle. "My mother's recipe book," he explained, pressing it into Maddie's hands. "Everything we know about preserving food, purifying water, living without power—it's all in there. She survived the Depression. Now it's your turn to survive this."

The distant wail of sirens mixed with another woman's scream. The smell of smoke grew stronger.

"Go, stay on 1A till you see signs for Route 1. You can take that to the interstate." Martha said firmly, but her voice cracked. "Go now, before we change our minds and keep you here forever."

Harold's bruised face was wet with tears as he opened the back door. "Head north," he instructed. "Stay off the main roads. And girls?" His voice caught. "Remember that there's still good in this world. You three—you're proof of that."

Martha pulled them in for one last group hug. "You're stronger than you know," she whispered. "All of you. Even you, Grace. Especially you."

As they wheeled their bikes toward the alley, Maddie looked back one last time. Martha and Harold stood in the doorway, silhouetted against the store's darkness, their hands clasped together. Two small figures standing against the chaos, choosing to be a light in the growing darkness.

Grace was sobbing openly now. Hannah wiped her eyes with Martha's handkerchief. And Maddie—Maddie felt something inside her shift, a determination taking root. If two elderly strangers could show such courage and kindness in the face of the apocalypse, maybe there was hope after all.

The last thing they heard as they pedaled away was Martha's voice, carried on the smoke-filled wind: "God go with you, my dears. God go with you."

Daniel

Lynnfield, Massachusetts—The Next Morning

A MORNING HEAT PRESSED AGAINST DANIEL'S SKIN as he woke, sweat already beading along his hairline. His hand instinctively reached for his phone before he remembered—a gesture as useless now as the device itself. Beside him, Jessica lay rigid, her eyes fixed on the ceiling, fingers worrying the edge of their Egyptian cotton sheets.

"Ready?" he asked, watching her jaw clench and release.

"The kids are already up." She turned to face him, dark circles betraying her sleepless night. Her usually perfectly styled hair lay tangled against the pillow. "I heard them whispering in the hallway. God, Daniel, how do we even begin to explain this?"

A floorboard creaked outside their room, followed by the soft padding of small feet and a badly suppressed giggle. Daniel pushed himself up, his muscles protesting after hours spent tossing and turning. The silence felt wrong—no whirring fans, no humming appliances, nothing but the unnaturally loud sound of birds outside their window.

They found Ryan and Lily huddled together on the family room couch, still in their pajamas. Ryan's shoulders hunched over his dead iPad, thumb jabbing repeatedly at the power button. His Spider-Man slippers tapped an anxious rhythm against the coffee table. Lily had pulled her knees up to her chest, Mr. Trunks squeezed tightly against her Frozen nightgown, her lower lip caught between her teeth—a sure sign she was fighting tears.

"Daddy!" Lily launched herself at him, her small body trembling. "Nothing works and I'm hungwy and—" Her voice hitched as she buried her face against his neck.

Daniel breathed in her baby shampoo scent, feeling her heart racing like a trapped bird. "Hey now," he murmured, running a hand over her tangled curls. "How about some breakfast? Mom can still make pancakes on the gas stove."

Ryan's head snapped up, hope flickering across his face before doubt crept back in. "But everything's broken," he said, his voice small and uncertain. He thrust the iPad forward, its black screen reflecting the morning light. "Fix it, Dad. You always fix everything."

The simple faith in those words hit Daniel like a physical blow. He swallowed hard, feeling Jessica's eyes on him as she moved toward the kitchen.

"How about chocolate chip pancakes first?" he deflected, carrying Lily toward the kitchen. She clung to him like she hadn't since she was a toddler, her stuffed elephant dragged behind them by one well-loved ear.

The kitchen—usually alive with the soft hum of their SubZero refrigerator and the glow of digital displays—felt eerily still. Jessica's hands shook slightly as she pulled out mixing bowls, the ceramic making too much noise against the marble countertop. She drew a steadying breath before speaking, her voice deliberately bright.

"Who wants to help measure flour?"

Lily lifted her head from Daniel's shoulder, tear tracks still visible on her cheeks. "Can I do the mixing part?"

"Of course, baby." Jessica's smile didn't quite reach her eyes as she helped Lily climb onto a bar stool. "Careful now, the bowl is heavy."

Through the window, Daniel watched their neighbor, Tom Peterson, trudging down the pristine sidewalk. The man's usual crisp appearance had crumbled—tie askew, shirt untucked, face drawn with confusion as his muscle memory reached repeatedly for a phone that wouldn't work.

Ryan abandoned his iPad on the couch and dragged himself to the kitchen island, chin propped on his hands. His dark hair stuck up in all directions, reminding Daniel painfully of his own father's perpetual bedhead. "Dad?" His voice wavered. "Why won't anything turn on?"

Daniel caught Jessica's eye over the children's heads. Her hands stilled in the pancake batter, waiting to hear how he'd explain this. He pulled out the bar stool next to Ryan, the legs scraping too loudly against the floor.

"Actually, guys, we need to talk about something exciting." Daniel forced enthusiasm into his voice, though his stomach churned. "How would you like to go on an adventure?"

Ryan's forehead crinkled, a mirror of Jessica's worried expression. "What kind of adventure?"

"We're going to visit Grandpa and Grandma's farm," Jessica jumped in, her wooden spoon moving with renewed vigor through the batter. A splash landed on her silk pajama top, but for once she didn't seem to notice.

Lily's eyes widened, her small fingers still clutched around Mr. Trunks. "The farm with the chickens?"

"That's right, Princess." Daniel reached over to wipe a smear of flour from her cheek. "And the big tractor, and the stream where we can catch frogs—"

"But what about my stuff?" Ryan sat up straighter, anxiety written across his face. "My Legos and my baseball cards and—" His lower lip started to tremble.

"We'll pack your favorite things," Jessica assured him quickly, though her knuckles were white around the mixing bowl. "Whatever fits in the truck."

Ryan's nose wrinkled. "The old truck? The stinky one in the garage?"

"It's not stinky!" Daniel defended automatically, though his mind was already cataloging everything he'd need to do to get it running. "It's… vintage."

Lily's face scrunched in confusion. "What's vintage mean?"

"It means old," Ryan informed her with all the authority his seven years could muster. "Like when Mom says her fancy shoes are classics but they're really just—"

"Who wants the first pancake?" Jessica interrupted, her face flushing slightly as she turned to the stove. The igniter would no longer work, and she struck a kitchen match to light the gas burners, accentuating the lack of power.

Daniel watched his family as they settled into the familiar rhythm of breakfast, noting every detail as if photographing it in his mind. The way Lily's feet swung under the counter, not quite reaching the footrest. The careful way Ryan cut his pancakes into precise squares, just like Jessica always did. The tremor in Jessica's hands as she poured more batter onto the griddle.

Through the kitchen window, he could see more neighbors emerging, gathering in small clusters on their manicured lawns. Someone was trying to start their Tesla, the futile clicking carrying across perfectly trimmed hedges. A sound that seemed to say: everything has changed, everything has changed, everything has changed.

"After breakfast," Daniel announced, pushing back from the counter, "I need to work on the truck. Ryan, want to help your old man?"

Ryan's face brightened for the first time that morning. "Can I use real tools?"

"We'll see." Daniel ruffled his son's hair, noticing how Ryan leaned into the touch, seeking comfort in the familiar gesture.

"Can I help, too?" Lily's voice quavered, her lower lip jutting out.

Jessica swooped in, gathering dirty plates with forced efficiency. "You can help me pack, Sweetie. We need to pick out which toys get to go on our adventure."

Daniel retreated to the garage, the morning heat already building. The '72 Ford sat waiting, its faded blue paint somehow reassuring in its imperfection. Unlike the gleaming Tesla next door, this was something he could fix with his hands, with tools and knowledge rather than computers.

He had the hood up and was elbow-deep in the engine when Ryan appeared, hovering in the doorway. His son had changed into play clothes, but his Spider-Man slippers remained, a small act of defiance against the strange new world.

"What can I do, Dad?"

Daniel pointed to his toolbox with a grease-stained hand. "Hand me that socket wrench. The big one."

Ryan's face scrunched in concentration as he dug through the tools, shoulders relaxing as he found purpose in the task. From inside the house came the sound of Lily's voice, rising in protest about something she couldn't bring, followed by Jessica's patient murmur.

The morning wore on in a blur of mechanical problems. A corroded fuel line crumbled in Daniel's hands. The starter motor groaned in protest. Each fix revealed another problem underneath, like picking at a scab only to find the wound still bleeding.

"Dad?" Ryan's voice pulled him from under the hood. "Can I go play with Tommy? He's outside with his bike."

Daniel straightened, his back protesting. Through the open garage door, he could see neighborhood kids gathering, their parents hovering nearby in small clusters. The children seemed to be adjusting faster than the adults, finding ways to play that didn't involve screens or electricity.

"Stay where I can see you," he said finally. "And take your sister."

Ryan's face fell. "But she's too little—"

"Ryan." Something in Daniel's tone must have conveyed the gravity of the situation, because his son's protest died unfinished.

Soon the sound of children playing filtered into the garage—their voices carrying clearly without the usual background hum of air conditioners and lawn equipment. Daniel kept one eye on them as he worked, watching Ryan show Lily how to ride without training wheels, their neighbor,

Tommy, making his own bike's siren noises since the electronic one no longer worked.

"The other kids say it's aliens!" Lily came running back, her cheeks flushed with excitement. "Tommy's big sister said they made all the phones stop working 'cause they're gonna take over!"

"Did not!" Ryan followed, trying to maintain his big-brother dignity despite being clearly unsettled by the idea. "Tommy's sister is stupid. Right, Dad? It's not really aliens?"

Before Daniel could answer, Jessica appeared in the doorway, her normally perfect hair pulled back in a messy ponytail. "Inside, both of you. It's too hot to be running around."

Daniel caught the real message in her tight expression—she'd seen something, heard something that worried her. The children's protests faded into the house as Jessica stepped into the garage, her voice dropping.

"The water pressure's getting worse," she reported, arms crossed tightly over her chest. "And I overheard the Petersons talking about looting at the mall in Burlington."

Daniel nodded grimly, wiping his hands on a rag. "How's the packing going?"

"The kids..." She swallowed hard. "They don't understand. They keep wanting to bring everything. Their whole lives are here, Daniel. Everything they know—"

Her voice broke. Daniel pulled her close, feeling her trembling against him. Over her shoulder, he could see their children through the window, Ryan now trying to teach Lily some complicated-looking hand clapping game. Their faces were serious with concentration, the game a lifeline to normalcy.

"The truck?" Jessica asked finally, pulling back to wipe her eyes.

"Getting there. But we need fuel." He nodded toward their Mercedes, sitting useless in the driveway. "I'll have to siphon what I can."

Jessica nodded, sending him back to his task saying, "I'll begin filling everything I can find before the water completely quits, while you finish up."

"Good thinking," Daniel said, eyeing the sky and a distant plume of smoke. "We might need it. You might want to start cooking everything that could spoil. I'll come help you when I finish up."

Wordlessly, she dipped her head and disappeared into the house where he heard her voice crack when asking the kids if they would like to play chefs.

The afternoon stretched on, marked by small victories and setbacks. The carburetor finally cooperated, but the brake lines looked suspicious. Jessica had organized their supplies into essential and non-essential piles, but decisions about what constituted "essential" sparked ongoing debate.

As evening approached, Austin Williams appeared in the garage doorway, looking less polished than usual without his morning shower. His casual weekend polo was wrinkled, his country club confidence wavering.

"Still playing with your toy truck, Thompson?" Austin's voice carried a sharp edge beneath its casual tone. He stepped into the garage, his movements too deliberate, too controlled.

His eyes darted from the tool chest to the workbench, cataloging contents in a way that made Daniel's neck prickle.

Daniel straightened slowly from the engine, aware of the heavy wrench in his hand. "Not playing, Austin. Working."

"Working?" Austin's laugh held no humor. Sweat darkened his polo shirt, and a muscle twitched near his jaw. "While the rest of us are trying to figure out when they're going to restore power, you're out here with this... this heap?" He gestured at the Ford with barely concealed contempt.

"They're not going to restore the power," Daniel said quietly, setting the wrench down but staying within reach of it.

"Of course they will." Austin stepped closer, his country club smile slipping. "They have to. Do you know how much I have tied up in the market right now? Millions in trades that need to clear. The system can't just... stop."

Daniel noticed Austin's hands flexing, clenching into fists before deliberately relaxing. Through the open garage door, he could see Ryan showing Lily how to do cartwheels on the lawn. Too close. Too exposed.

"Ryan," he called out, keeping his eyes on Austin. "Take your sister inside. Help Mom with packing."

"But Dad—"

"Now, Buddy."

Something in his tone made Ryan grab Lily's hand without further protest, hurrying her toward the house despite her complaints about interrupted cartwheel practice.

Austin watched them go, his expression darkening. "Packing? You're actually leaving? Walking away from all this?" He gestured at their manicured neighborhood, his voice rising. "For what? Some family farm in the middle of nowhere?"

"That's the plan. We figure it is a good time to go visit, anyway."

"The plan?" Austin stepped closer, invading Daniel's space. His cologne—probably worth more than the old Ford's entire engine—couldn't quite mask the sour smell of fear-sweat. "Let me tell you about plans, Thompson. I had plans. Big plans. And I didn't get where I am by running away when things got tough."

Daniel shifted, angling himself between Austin and the toolbox. "This isn't a downturn in the market, Austin. This is different."

"Different?" Austin's fingers drummed against his thigh—the same nervous gesture he made during tense client meetings. "You know what's different? You. Standing out here playing mechanic while the rest of us are trying to hold things together. Acting like you know something we don't."

The accusation hung in the air between them. Daniel caught movement in his peripheral vision—Jessica in the doorway, then quickly pulling back inside. Good. She'd seen something was wrong.

"You do know something, don't you?" Austin's voice dropped to a near-whisper. "Your father called you yesterday. Right before everything went dark. What did he tell you?"

Daniel said nothing, but his eyes flicked involuntarily to the gas can he'd been using to siphon fuel from the Mercedes.

Austin followed his gaze. "That's it, isn't it? You're not just leaving. You're taking resources. Stealing fuel while the rest of us—" He cut himself off, a cold smile spreading across his face. "You always were the quiet one at the club. Always watching, planning. Well, let me tell you something—"

"Dad?" Ryan's voice from the doorway made them both turn. "Mom says to come in. She needs help with something heavy."

Daniel silently thanked Jessica's quick thinking. "Be right there, Buddy." He turned back to Austin, keeping his voice level. "I think we're done here."

Austin stepped back, his country club manner sliding back into place like a mask. But his eyes were different now—harder, calculating. "Sure, Thompson. We're done. For now." He turned to leave, then paused. "Just remember—when nothing gets fixed, when no help comes—remember who your real neighbors are. Remember who knows where you live."

Daniel watched him walk away, noting how other neighbors quickly found reasons to go inside as Austin passed. Through the kitchen window, he could see Jessica hovering, phone clutched uselessly in her hand—an instinct to call for help that could no longer be fulfilled.

The wrench felt very cold against his palm as he realized Austin wasn't just angry or scared. He was dangerous. And he wasn't the only one who would be watching the old Ford take shape, counting supplies, making plans of their own.

Daniel turned back to the truck with renewed urgency. They needed to leave. Soon. Before neighbors became threats, before desperate people started doing desperate things.

Before Austin's thinly veiled warning became a promise.

James

The Day After—Cornish, Maine

THIS MORNING ALREADY HAD AN UNSETTLING FEEL about it as James sat at the kitchen bar, watching dawn creep across his fields. The morning light painted everything in harsh clarity—too bright, too real, as if the world had shed some protective filter overnight. His coffee had gone cold, the bitter dregs settling in the metal camping mug Sarah had dug out after realizing their electric coffee maker was now just expensive kitchen décor.

"The guest room sheets need changing," Sarah announced, bustling into the kitchen with an armload of linens. "Elena shouldn't sleep on anything less than the Egyptian cotton set. She needs to stay comfortable, especially now."

James watched his wife's determined domesticity with a mixture of love and worry. She'd been up since before dawn, scrubbing and organizing as if preparing for a holiday gathering rather than surviving an apocalypse.

"Sarah," he began gently, "maybe we should focus on—"

"And we'll need to rearrange the pantry," she continued, refusing to meet his eyes. "Matthew said Elena's been craving those apple butter preserves I made last fall. Thank goodness we still have a few jars left."

The sound of retching drifted down from upstairs, followed by Matthew's anxious voice: "Mom? MOM! Elena's sick again!"

Sarah dropped the sheets and hurried toward the stairs, her bare feet silent on the wooden floors. James watched her go, noting how she'd already changed into her "company clothes"—pressed slacks and a neat blouse, as if the power company might show up any minute to restore their normal life.

Emily appeared in the doorway, dark circles under her eyes suggesting she'd barely slept. "The kids are still asleep," she reported quietly. "Michael's checking the perimeter again. He's… worried about security."

A sharp rap at the back door made them both jump. Frank Wilson—"Boozer" to most of the town—stood on the other side of the screen, his usual dishevelment now tinged with something darker. His eyes darted between James and Emily, calculating in a way that set James's teeth on edge.

"Thompson," Frank called through the screen, his voice carrying a forced cheerfulness that didn't match his expression. "Thought we might want to discuss arrangements. You know, community organization and all that."

James felt Emily tense beside him. Frank's reputation for helping himself to others' property was well-known, usually ignored as a quirk of small-town life. But now…

"Kind of early for social calls, Frank," James replied carefully, not moving to open the door.

Frank's laugh held no humor. "Early? Hell, Thompson, time's wasting. Got half the town without water pressure already. People are getting scared. Getting desperate." He leaned closer to the screen, lowering his voice. "But you've got that generator in the barn. Got those solar panels old Jenkins helped you install. Got all this land, all these resources…"

The way he emphasized "resources" made James's hand tighten on his coffee mug. Through the screen door, he could smell alcohol on Frank's breath—apparently some supplies hadn't been disrupted by the CME.

"We'll call a proper town meeting," James said firmly. "Get everyone together, figure things out properly."

Frank's expression shifted, something ugly flickering behind his eyes. "A meeting? While people are suffering? While kids are going hungry? That's cold, Thompson. Real cold." He straightened, adjusting his worn jacket with exaggerated dignity. "Just remember—people talk. And they're already talking about how the Thompsons always seem to land on their feet while others struggle."

The threat hung in the air between them, made worse by its vague delivery. Emily moved closer to James, her nurse's training evident in how she positioned herself to help if needed.

"Guess I'll see myself out," Frank announced, too loudly. "But we'll talk again soon. Real soon."

They watched him swagger down the drive, his path weaving slightly—drunk before sunrise, James realized with a mix of pity and disgust.

"Dad?" Matthew's voice carried down the stairs, edged with panic. "Elena's really sick. We need help!"

James met Emily's eyes, seeing his own worry reflected there. The world had changed overnight, but family still came first. They would deal with Frank Wilson and his threats later.

For now, there were animals to feed, equipment to check, and a pregnant woman who needed their help. The sun climbed higher, harsh and unforgiving, as James headed toward the barn to start another day in this strange new world.

The real question wasn't whether Frank would be back—it was what and who he'd bring with him when he did.

Michael pushed through the screen door, his jaw tight. "Frank's making the rounds," he reported, running a hand through his close-cropped hair. "Saw him stumbling toward the Miller place. Already got Old Man Jenkins worked up about 'community resources'."

James snorted, though the knot in his stomach tightened. "Frank Wilson looking out for the community? That'll be the day." He set his coffee mug in the sink, the metal clinking against porcelain. "He's just playing at being in charge. We all know who Frank really looks out for."

"Still," Michael's bearing remained rigid, "people are scared. And Frank's good at exploiting that."

Sarah's voice carried from the kitchen, bright and brittle: "Breakfast in fifteen minutes! I'm making those biscuits everyone loves." The sound of her aggressive whisking echoed through the house. "Oh! And we should set extra places. Daniel and the family might arrive while we're eating, and we can't have a proper family dinner without them."

The silence that followed her announcement felt heavy, oppressive. James caught Michael's questioning look as they headed toward the back door.

"She's..." James began, then stopped, searching for words as they stepped into the morning air. "She can't accept it. Not yet. And Daniel..." His voice caught slightly. "God, Michael, they're in Lynnfield. Right outside Boston. If the city's as bad as Jenkins says..."

Michael clasped his father-in-law's shoulder. "Daniel's

smart. He'll get them out if he can."

"If he can," James echoed, the words bitter in his mouth. They walked toward the barn in silence, the gravel crunching under their boots. The morning sun felt too bright, too harsh, highlighting every imperfection in their once-ordinary world.

Behind them, Sarah's voice drifted through the open windows, humming as she prepared a breakfast for family members who might never arrive.

The barn door protested as James heaved it open, hinges crying out for oil he'd been meaning to apply for weeks. Morning light slanted through dust motes, illuminating the organized chaos within—tools hanging in their assigned places, hay bales stacked against the far wall, the ancient tractor squatting in its corner like some mechanical beast at rest.

"Generator's still good," Michael reported, checking the equipment with practiced efficiency. "But we're going to need to be smart about fuel. Even with the reserve tanks, we've got maybe two weeks at most."

James nodded, moving toward the animals. The horses nickered softly in greeting, sensing his approach. At least they still had the manual pump for the water trough—his grandfather's insistence on keeping the old equipment suddenly seemed prescient rather than stubborn.

"At least the power tools still work," Michael said, testing the battery-powered drill. The whir of the motor seemed unnaturally loud in the quiet barn. "But we'll need to be careful with the batteries. Once they're dead…" He glanced toward the roof. "Solar panels might help, but without working charge controllers…"

James nodded, understanding the unspoken concern. They had power for now, but like everything else, it was finite. "One problem at a time," he said, setting the drill back in its place. "Let's not borrow trouble just yet."

A crash from the storage room made them both jump. James grabbed a pitchfork before he could stop himself, while Michael's hand went instinctively to where his service weapon would have been. A fat raccoon burst from behind some feed sacks, scampering toward the door.

"Hell," James breathed, lowering the pitchfork. "Getting jumpy already."

Michael's laugh held no humor. "Better jumpy than sorry." He moved to check the feed sacks for damage. "We need to think about security, James. Real security. Frank's not the only one who's going to come looking once things get bad."

"Things are already bad," James corrected, running a hand along the horse's flank. The animal's warmth felt reassuring, real. "Question is, how do we keep them from getting worse?"

"We need inventory," Michael said, being systematic in his approach. "Everything useful, everything essential. We need to know what we have before we can plan how to defend it."

James watched his son-in-law move through the barn, noting items with the precision of someone used to evaluating tactical situations. Michael had always seemed almost too serious for Emily, too rigid for their family's easy-going ways. Now that rigidity felt like an anchor in choppy seas.

"Sarah's not the only one in denial," Michael said quietly, pausing by the old manual tools. "Matthew's useless—totally focused on Elena. Emily's trying to hold everyone together. And you…" He turned to face his father-in-law. "You're still trying to be the good neighbor, the community leader. But this isn't a town council meeting we're planning for. This is survival."

The words hung in the dusty air between them. Outside, a rooster crowed—something so normal it felt almost obscene in their new reality.

"Daniel could handle this," James said finally, the words coming unbidden. "He always had a knack for seeing the bigger picture, for planning ahead. If he's alive—if he can get his family here…"

"When," Michael corrected firmly. "When he gets here." He moved closer, lowering his voice though they were alone in the barn. "But James, we need to be ready. For whatever comes first—Daniel's family, or Frank's kind of trouble."

The screen door slapped against its frame, and Sarah's voice carried across the yard: "Breakfast! Come on now, before it gets cold!"

James exchanged a look with Michael. They had a hundred concerns to address, a thousand decisions to make, but maybe they could allow themselves this one normal moment first.

"We'll figure it out after breakfast," James said, brushing hay from his jeans. "Right now, let's just… let's just be family."

Michael nodded, his stern look softening slightly. "Emily says sometimes you have to put the crisis aside, just for a minute. To remember what you're fighting for."

They walked back toward the house together, the morning sun warming their shoulders. Through the kitchen window, they could see Sarah arranging biscuits on her best serving plate, Emily helping her lay out the table settings with careful precision. The scene was so ordinary, so precious in its normalcy, that James felt his throat tighten.

For just a little while, they could pretend this was any other summer morning on the farm. The hard decisions, the preparations, Frank's threats—they would keep for an hour while the family broke bread together. Even if some chairs remained emptier than Sarah wanted to admit.

The kitchen smelled of fresh biscuits and coffee brewed over the gas stove. Sarah had set the table with her good china—the plates with the delicate blue flowers that usually only came out for Christmas dinner. Emily helped Elena settle into a chair, the pregnant woman's face still pale from her morning sickness.

"I made extra," Sarah announced, setting a heaping platter of biscuits in the center of the table. "In case Daniel and the kids arrive during breakfast." She smoothed her apron, eyes darting to the empty chairs. "And there's plenty of apple butter. Elena's favorite."

Matthew stabbed at his biscuit with unnecessary force. "Mom, stop. Just… stop."

"Stop what?" Sarah's voice maintained its bright tone, though her hands trembled slightly as she poured coffee. "I'm simply being prepared. A good hostess always—"

"Hostess?" Matthew's laugh held an edge of hysteria. "Mom, the world is literally falling apart. There's no power, no phones, no internet. Elena can barely keep food down, and we can't even call her doctor. Nothing's normal anymore. Nothing will ever be normal again!"

The coffee pot slipped in Sarah's hands, dark liquid splashing across her pristine tablecloth. She stared at the spreading stain as if it had personally betrayed her.

"Matthew," Emily warned softly, but he was too far gone.

"And Daniel? God, Mom, he's probably…" Matthew's voice cracked. "Boston's probably a war zone by now. But you're setting places for them like… Like it's Sunday dinner?

Like everything's fine?"

"It will be fine," Sarah insisted, her voice rising. "Once the power comes back—"

"It's not coming back!" Matthew slammed his hand on the table, making the china rattle. "This isn't a storm outage. This isn't—"

The sound of breaking china cut through the air like a gunshot. Sarah's plate lay shattered on the floor, blue flowers scattered across white tiles. Her chest heaved as she stared at the mess, something wild and terrible breaking across her face.

"You think I don't know?" she screamed, her composure finally shattering like the china at her feet. "You think I don't understand?" Her voice climbed higher, decades of motherly restraint crumbling. "My baby is out there somewhere! My grandbabies! But I can't—I can't—"

The last word dissolved into a sob. She turned and fled, her footsteps pounding up the stairs. A door slammed overhead, the sound echoing through the suddenly silent house.

Elena began to cry quietly, her hands protectively cradling her belly. Matthew deflated, all his anger turning to shame as he reached for his girlfriend's shoulder.

James stood slowly, the weight of his family's fear pressing against his chest like a physical thing. Emily was already moving to clean up the broken china, her gentle efficiency a stark contrast to the chaos of moments before.

"I'll go," Michael said quietly, touching James's arm. "You stay. Sometimes it's easier to break down with someone who isn't quite as close to the pain."

James watched his son-in-law climb the stairs, remembering how he'd once worried Michael was too rigid for their family. Now his quiet strength seemed like exactly what they needed.

Through the window, the morning sun continued its relentless climb, indifferent to their small human dramas. Somewhere out there, Daniel and his family were trying to survive. But here, in this kitchen, James could only hold the pieces of china he'd retrieved from beneath the table. Sarah'd always been so careful with it. Thirty-Seven years of marriage and not a nick; this one plate punctuated the reality they now faced. Their very world had been shattered.

Maddie

North of Boston, Massachusetts

THE BIKE'S METAL FRAME BURNED HOT AGAINST Maddie's thighs as she pedaled through the smoke-filled streets of East Boston. Each rotation of the wheels crunched broken glass beneath them, the sound unnaturally loud in the morning quiet. Sweat traced lines down her back, soaking through the light tank top Martha had insisted she take. The old woman's handkerchief was tied around her neck, ready to pull up against the smoke if needed.

They followed Route 1A as Martha suggested they do, but the maze of destroyed vehicles and debris forced them to weave through side streets. Each detour pushed them further from their intended path until the familiar landmarks disappeared entirely.

"I think we're going the wrong way," Hannah called out, her medical bag bouncing against her hip as she pedaled. "The water should be on our right."

Maddie scanned their surroundings, trying to orient herself. The morning sun offered no help, obscured by thick smoke that turned the sky into an oppressive ceiling. "There," she pointed toward a break in the buildings. "I see marsh grass."

They cut through a parking lot, emerging onto a service road that bordered Rumney Marsh. The vast expanse of wetland stretched before them, surprisingly peaceful compared to the chaos they'd left behind. Tall grass swayed in the hot breeze, and somewhere, a bird called out - nature indifferent to humanity's collapse.

"At least it's quiet," Grace whispered, her knuckles white on her handlebars.

They followed the marsh's edge, the cracked but clear sidewalk pavement easier to navigate than debris-strewn streets. The July heat pressed down mercilessly, but here the air felt cleaner, carrying the brackish scent of mud and salt water instead of smoke and fear.

An hour passed as they slowed their pace and paused for a break in relative silence, broken only by the soft whir of bike chains and their labored breathing. The marsh gradually gave way to more developed areas, and suddenly they were emerging onto Western Avenue, the massive bulk of the GE plant looming ahead like a steel mountain.

"Lynn," Hannah breathed. "We made it to Lynn."

They pedaled along Western Ave, picking up speed as they went further into the city. Something crashed a few blocks over, making Grace yelp. The sound cut off as abruptly as it had started, leaving them frozen in the street.

"Which way?" Grace asked, her voice trembling.

Maddie hesitated at the intersection of Franklin Street. Right would keep them parallel to the coast, but something - instinct maybe, or just fear of the open road - made her turn left. They pedaled quickly down Franklin, taking a right onto Boston Street that seemed to head in their general direction.

The mistake became apparent as they approached Pine Grove Cemetery. A group of men were systematically looting the strip of stores across the street, their shouts clear in the morning air.

"Back up," Maddie hissed, but it was too late.

"Hey! Over there!"

The girls turned their bikes sharply, pushing through the cemetery's open gates. Headstones blurred past as they pedaled desperately uphill into the rows between ancient gravestones seeking another exit. Behind them, engines roared to life - their pursuers had vehicles.

"Up there!" Hannah pointed toward a rise in the cemetery crowned with larger monuments. "We can see where we're going!"

They abandoned their bikes behind a massive granite tomb, crouching in its shadow. Grace's breathing came in sharp gasps as vehicles prowled the cemetery roads below.

"Over here." Maddie pulled them behind a larger monument, its weathered angel providing better cover. From this vantage point, they could see all the way back to Boston. Columns of smoke rose from multiple points in the city, dark smudges against the hazy sky that marked civilization's retreat.

Grace's legs gave out, and she slid to the ground, her face crumpling. "I can't," she sobbed, but quietly now - fear had taught her that much. "I can't do this anymore."

Hannah kneeled beside her while Maddie kept watch. Below, car doors slammed as their pursuers began searching on foot.

Grace's control shattered completely then, her quiet whimper building into wracking sobs. "Nothing makes sense anymore," she gasped between heaving breaths. "There's no internet, no phones, no anything. People are trying to kill us and everything's burning and—"

"Shh!" Hannah tried to quiet her, but Grace was beyond reach.

"I don't want to die!" Her voice rose dangerously. "I don't want to die in some stupid cemetery because the world ended and—"

Maddie moved fast, clamping a hand over Grace's mouth. The younger girl thrashed against her grip, tears streaming down her face. Below, voices carried up the hill:

"You hear something?"

"Check the mausoleums. Could be hiding anywhere in this maze."

Grace's scream caught behind Maddie's palm, transforming into a muffled keen. Hannah wrapped her arms around the girl from behind, whispering soothing nonsense into her hair until the fight slowly drained from her body.

When Grace finally went limp, Maddie carefully removed her hand. The younger girl curled into herself, shoulders shaking with silent sobs. Hannah kept hold of her while Maddie crept to the edge of their hiding spot, watching their pursuers systematically search the lower sections of the cemetery.

"We need to move soon," Maddie whispered, "but they've got the main paths covered."

"She needs rest," Hannah said softly. "We all do. And food." She glanced at Grace's huddled form. "The heat and stress… we're all dehydrated."

Maddie nodded reluctantly. The morning's exertion had left them drained, and the July sun beat down mercilessly on the exposed hilltop. She dug through her pack, pulling out the water and preserved meat Martha had insisted they take.

They ate in tense silence, passing a water bottle between them. Grace managed a few small bites before curling up in the monument's shadow, exhaustion finally overwhelming her terror. Her face, even in sleep, remained twisted with anxiety.

Hannah moved closer to Maddie, her voice barely a whisper. "This is getting worse."

"I know." Maddie watched another column of smoke rise from distant Boston. "The cracks in society are getting more frequent. Louder. People area already getting desperate."

"She's going to get us killed." Hannah's blunt assessment carried no malice, just medical precision. "Or herself. You saw her back there—she completely lost control. If you hadn't covered her mouth…"

"What are we supposed to do?" Maddie turned to her friend. "Leave her behind?"

"Of course not." Hannah's medical bag lay open beside her, its contents meticulously organized despite their flight. "But we need a plan. She's not processing any of this. The denial, the hysteria—it's escalating. And we're not even halfway home."

Maddie pulled Martha's handkerchief from around her neck, twisting it between her fingers. "She's just scared. We're all scared."

"This is different." Hannah's voice remained clinical, but her hands shook slightly as she repacked her bag. "You and I, we're dealing with the fear. Processing it. Grace is…" She paused, choosing her words carefully. "Grace is fracturing. Each new trauma, each moment of violence compounding on the others. They're hitting her like physical blows. And she's not bouncing back anymore."

Below them, a car door slammed. Their pursuers were regrouping, but hadn't yet started up the hill. Maddie watched them through gaps in the weathered granite, her mind racing.

"We need to get her home," she said finally. "To her parents. To something familiar. She just needs—"

"Home might not exist anymore," Hannah cut her off gently. "Not the way she remembers it. Not the way any of us remember it." She touched Maddie's arm. "And what happens when she realizes that? When we get there and everything's changed?"

Maddie checked their pursuers' positions one last time before starting to pack up their supplies. The sun had moved past its zenith, and they needed to move while they still had decent light.

"This is going to make such an amazing TikTok series," Grace chirped, smoothing her hair with trembling hands. The sudden shift in her demeanor made Maddie's stomach clench. "I mean, the aesthetics alone—all that smoke over Boston? So…apocalyptic-chic. O-M-G I just thought up the next trending hashtag. My followers are going to absolutely die."

Hannah shot Maddie a worried look as she repacked her medical bag. Grace continued, her voice taking on an odd, sing-song quality.

"I should start planning my posts now. Maybe do a whole survival-fashion thing? 'What I Wore During the Apocalypse'—that would totally trend." She giggled; the sound unnaturally high. "And wait until I tell everyone about Martha and Harold! Such an amazing human interest moment. The audience will eat it up."

"Grace," Hannah started, but Maddie shook her head slightly. This chattering Grace was easier to manage than the screaming one.

"Oh! And I can do one of those 'Day in the Life' reels about biking through everything. You know, add some moody music, maybe that sound that's going viral right now—" She hummed a few bars of something, swaying slightly. "Though I should probably wait for better lighting. The golden hour will really make the burning buildings pop."

Maddie methodically redistributed their supplies between the packs, watching Grace from the corner of her eye. The younger girl was now typing on her dead phone with absolute conviction, muttering about hashtags and engagement metrics.

"We need to move soon," Hannah whispered, crouching beside Maddie. "The searchers have moved toward the west side. If we time it right…"

"I know." Maddie zipped up her pack. "But quietly. No sudden moves that might…" She glanced at Grace, who was now taking selfies with her blank phone screen.

"This will make such a great story highlight," Grace announced, her voice still maintaining that strange, bright tone. "I bet I'll get verified after this. Maybe even sponsorship deals! Can you imagine? 'This apocalyptic breakdown brought to you by—"

"Grace." Maddie kept her voice gentle but firm. "We need to move now. Very quietly."

"Oh! Behind the scenes content!" Grace nodded enthusiastically, lowering her voice to a stage whisper. "My followers love that. So authentic."

They gathered their bikes, Grace still narrating everything in influencer-speak. Maddie found herself almost missing the hysteria—at least that had been rooted in reality. This smiling, chattering version of Grace felt like watching someone sleep walk along the edge of a cliff.

"The thing about content creation," Grace continued as they carefully walked their bikes between the monuments, "is that you have to stay on brand. And honestly? This whole 'end of civilization' thing? Amazing rebrand opportunity. So much room for…" her voice trailed off as she held the dead phone over her head, making a peace sign with two fingers for the imaginary selfie.

Hannah's hand clamped over Grace's mouth as voices carried up from nearby. They froze behind a large family plot, Grace's eyes wide but still somehow vacant above Hannah's fingers. When the voices passed, she just giggled softly and mimed zipping her lips.

"Good ASMR moment," she whispered. "Very tension-building."

Maddie caught Hannah's eye as they began moving again. They shared a look of understanding—Grace wasn't better. She was worse. Much worse. But at least this version of worse was quiet enough to keep them alive.

For now.

They crept down the hill's eastern slope, using the larger monuments for cover. Maddie led the way, each step calculated, while Hannah kept one hand on Grace's arm to steady her. Their bikes made the going treacherous, wheels catching on exposed roots and ancient grave markers.

"This lighting is everything," Grace whispered, still clutching her dead phone. "Very 'survivor-core.' Should I do a quick outfit transition video? You know, before and after the apocalypse? Though my hair is totally—"

"Shh," Maddie hissed, spotting movement below. Two men with rifles crossed between mausoleums, scanning the grounds. She waited until they passed before motioning the others forward.

"The tension!" Grace's whisper carried an edge of hysteria beneath its forced perkiness. "My followers are going to be so invested. Like, comment and subscribe if you've ever had to hide from looters! Don't forget to hit that notification bell—"

Hannah's grip on Grace's arm tightened. "Grace, honey, we need absolute quiet now."

"Behind the scenes content," Grace nodded sagely, but her voice dropped even lower. "Very exclusive. Patreon-only material."

They reached the cemetery's eastern wall – old brick, crumbling in places. Beyond it lay a residential street that seemed mercifully empty. Maddie pressed herself against the sun-warmed brick, considering their options.

"This would be perfect for a sponsored segment," Grace continued, her voice dreamy. "Today's escape route brought to you by—"

The crack of a rifle shot cut through the air. They dropped instinctively, Grace's commentary dissolving into a giggle that scared Maddie more than screams would have.

"Amazing sound effect," Grace whispered. "So authentic. The production value—"

"There! By the wall!" A shout from their right. Too close.

"We have to move. Now." Maddie spotted a section of wall where decades of frost heave had created a gap beneath it. "Hannah, you first. Then Grace."

Hannah slid her bike under the wall, then herself, drawing

a sharp breath as broken brick scraped her back. Grace went next, still mumbling about camera angles and engagement metrics. Another shot rang out, closer, sending chips of brick flying.

"Hurry!" Hannah pulled Grace clear of the wall.

Maddie shoved her bike through, then started to follow. Something hot sliced across her upper arm – a bullet grazing brick, or the brick itself exploding. She bit back a cry as she tumbled through the gap.

"That's definitely going viral," Grace said cheerfully as Hannah yanked her onto her bike. "The cinematography alone—"

"Pedal!" Maddie ordered, swinging onto her own bike. Blood trickled down her arm, but there was no time to check the damage. "Now!"

They flew down the residential street, Grace providing running commentary between gasping breaths: "Don't forget… to like and… subscribe! Link in bio… for more survival… content!"

Behind them, engines roared to life. Their pursuers had realized they'd escaped and were mobilizing. Maddie's mind raced – they needed somewhere to hide, somewhere to regroup. Her arm throbbed with each rotation of the pedals.

"Next week's video," Grace called out, her voice growing shriller, "we'll do a full breakdown of proper bug-out bag essentials! But first, a word from our sponsors—"

A truck engine growled somewhere ahead. They were about to be boxed in.

"This way!" Maddie cut left between houses, hoping the narrow spaces would work to their advantage. Behind them,

Grace's social media monologue continued, becoming more fractured with each passing moment.

They burst out onto a main street, the sounds of pursuit growing closer, when Maddie spotted it – a massive tangle of abandoned vehicles completely blocking the intersection ahead. Cars were wedged together at impossible angles, creating a barricade their pursuers' trucks couldn't hope to navigate.

"Through there!" she called out, spotting narrow gaps between the wreckage. "Quick!"

They threaded their bikes through the maze of twisted metal, Grace still chattering about "aesthetic urban decay shots" and "perfect thumbnail opportunities." The sound of engines cut off behind them – their pursuers had reached the blockade.

"Can't get through there," a distant voice shouted. "They're heading toward Route One!"

A road sign, bent but readable, pointed left: ROUTE 1 NORTH.

"This way," Maddie gasped, her arm still bleeding. They turned onto Lynnfield Street, pedaling hard. The road stretched ahead of them, relatively clear compared to what they'd left behind. Grace's commentary had devolved into disconnected social media phrases.

"Like… comment… don't forget to… ring that bell"

They rode fast, the late afternoon sun at their backs casting long shadows ahead of them. Buildings thinned out, giving way to more open spaces. Then suddenly, looming ahead – a massive overhead sign spanning the rotary: I-95 NORTH.

"Follow the signs," Hannah called out, "we need to stop soon – check that arm."

They navigated the rotary, finding the on-ramp to the

highway. The elevated road offered a clear view of their surroundings – cars abandoned in eerie stillness, but no movement. No people. Just the distant smoke of Boston behind them and the promise of home ahead.

They wheeled their bikes into the small wooded area between the on-ramp and the highway, finding refuge in the shade of scrubby pines. The late afternoon sun filtered through the branches, casting dappled shadows on the patchy grass beneath. The steady drone of cicadas had returned, nature's rhythm continuing despite everything.

"Sit," Hannah ordered, already digging through her medical bag. "That arm needs attention."

Maddie sank onto a fallen log, the adrenaline fade making her limbs feel heavy. The graze on her arm looked worse than it was – more scraped by exploding brick than bullet, but it still bled freely.

Grace perched on a rock nearby, her fingers moving across her dead phone's screen in practiced swipes. "Should I do a first aid tutorial?" she asked no one in particular. "Those always get good engagement. Though the lighting in these trees isn't ideal for—"

"Stay still," Hannah murmured as she cleaned Maddie's wound. Her hands were steady, professional, but her voice shook slightly. "We got lucky. A few inches to the left…"

Through gaps in the trees, they could see cars scattered across the highway like abandoned toys. The road stretched north, a dark ribbon disappearing into the summer haze. Grace had started taking selfies again with her blank phone. "Perfect backdrop," she whispered. "Very survival-chic. Just need to edit out the blood…"

The antiseptic stung, making Maddie hiss through her

teeth. Hannah's hands paused. "Sorry."

"It's fine." Maddie's eyes stayed on Grace. "We can't stay here long."

"Long enough to do this properly." Hannah began wrapping gauze around Maddie's arm with practiced efficiency. "We need you functional."

Far off in the distance, gunshots rang out and then silence. Grace hummed tunelessly, lost in her imaginary social media world.

"And that's it for today's video," she announced to the empty air. "Don't forget to follow for more apocalypse survival content. Link in bio for my exclusive prepper merch line…"

Hannah tied off the bandage, her touch lingering on Maddie's arm. They shared a look of understanding—they were alone now, really alone, in shepherding their fractured friend toward a home that might no longer exist.

"Next up on the channel," Grace continued dreamily, "we'll be reviewing the top ten must-have items for your elite survival squad. But first, a word from our sponsors…"

Beyond their wooded shelter, the highway waited with its maze of abandoned vehicles stretching toward whatever remained of the world they'd known. And Grace, still typing on her dead phone, smiled at nothing at all.

Lynnfield, Massachusetts—Day Two Post CME

THE MORNING SUNLIGHT FILTERED THROUGH THE kitchen windows, casting long shadows across their marble countertops. Daniel sat at the island, watching his family pick at the remains of their breakfast. The gas stove had allowed Jessica to make pancakes again, though the batter was noticeably thinner than yesterday—she was rationing the milk.

"The transformers were quieter last night," Daniel said deliberately, catching Jessica's eye as he spoke. "Probably means they're fixing them. I'd bet we'll have power back any day now."

Ryan's head snapped up from his plate, hope blazing across his face. "Really? So I can play Minecraft again soon?"

"Sure thing, buddy." Daniel forced a smile, noting how Jessica's hands trembled slightly as she gathered the dishes. "Probably just a matter of days before everything's back to normal."

Lily hugged Mr. Trunks closer, her voice small but excited. "Then we don't have to go on the trip?"

"Well," Daniel stretched the word out, watching his children's reactions carefully, "maybe we'll postpone our little *vacation*." He emphasized the last word meaningfully, seeing

Jessica's slight nod of understanding. "After all, no sense driving all the way to Maine when I'll need to be back at work soon, right?"

A sharp knock at the front door made them all jump. Austin's voice carried through clearly: "Thompson! You up? We need to talk!"

Daniel caught Jessica's eye, tilting his head slightly toward the back stairs. She nodded, already gathering the children. "Come on, you two. Let's get dressed for the day."

"But Daddy—" Lily started to protest.

"Go with Mom, Princess." Daniel kept his voice light. "I just need to have a boring grown-up conversation about work stuff."

He waited until his family had disappeared upstairs before opening the front door, plastering a surprised smile on his face. "Austin! I was just telling the kids I bet we'll have power back any day now. What do you think?"

Austin stood on the porch, his country club casualness slightly frayed around the edges. His polo shirt was wrinkled, and his normally perfect hair showed signs of manual styling without product. "That's… that's what you think?"

"Come in, come in." Daniel ushered him inside, noting the way Austin's eyes darted around the kitchen, taking inventory. "Jessica just made coffee on the gas stove. Want a cup?"

"Coffee?" Something in Austin's rigid posture softened slightly. "Real coffee?"

"French press," Daniel confirmed, moving to pour a cup. "Not as good as our usual espresso machine, but it'll do until the power's back." He watched Austin sink onto a bar stool, hands wrapping around the offered mug. "Noticed the transformer explosions died down last night. Good sign, right?"

Austin took a long sip, something desperate in the gesture. "You really think they're fixing things?"

"Have to be." Daniel leaned against the counter, the picture of casual confidence. "I mean, this is Massachusetts, not some third-world country. They've probably got crews working round the clock." He chuckled. "Though I have to admit, this forced downtime isn't all bad. When was the last time we actually had a morning free to just… relax?"

"Relax?" Austin's laugh held a hysterical edge. "Daniel, I have millions in trades pending—"

"Which will process as soon as systems are back online," Daniel cut in smoothly. "Look at it this way—we're basically getting a free vacation. Hey, speaking of which—" He gestured toward the garage, his expression deliberately sheepish. "I don't suppose you know anything about old trucks? That damn thing in there is driving me crazy."

Austin's posture shifted subtly. "The Ford? I thought you were—" He caught himself. "I mean, I noticed you working on it yesterday."

"Yeah, my therapist said I needed a hobby." Daniel rolled his eyes dramatically. "Should've taken up golf instead. Every time I think I fix something, three more problems pop up. Starting to think it's a lost cause."

He could almost see the calculations running behind Austin's eyes—the truck that had seemed so threatening yesterday now recast as just another rich man's failed project.

"Actually," Daniel continued, warming to his performance, "since we're stuck here anyway—what do you say to hitting some balls later? That empty field behind the Peterson place would work. Better than letting our swings get rusty while we wait for the club to reopen."

Austin's smile became more genuine. "Could be fun. I've got some balls in my garage." He stood, setting his empty coffee cup down. "You know, Thompson, I think I might have misjudged things yesterday. This situation has everyone on edge."

"Hey, no harm done." Daniel walked him to the door. "We're all just trying to figure things out. But look at it this way—when was the last time you had a guilt-free excuse to play hooky from the office?"

As Austin headed home, Daniel maintained his relaxed smile until the door closed. Only then did he allow his shoulders to sag, the performance dropping away.

"That was impressive," Jessica's voice came softly from the stairs. "I almost believed you myself."

Daniel turned to find his wife watching him, Lily's favorite stuffed animals piled in her arms. "Did you finish packing their things?"

She nodded, her eyes worried. "How long do we have to keep pretending?"

"Just until the truck's ready." He moved to help her with the stuffed animals. "Another day, maybe two. Just enough time to convince everyone we're settling in for a long power outage, nothing more." He glanced out the window, where Austin was already spreading the word to other neighbors, gesturing animatedly. "Let them think we're all just waiting it out together. It'll be easier to leave if they're not watching for it."

"Daddy!" Lily's voice carried down the stairs. "Can we play outside? Please?"

"Sure, Princess." He raised his voice to carry upstairs. "But stay in the yard where I can see you!"

Jessica's hand found his, squeezing gently. "You're good at this," she whispered. "The misdirection, the performance."

"I spent fifteen years convincing people to trust me with their money," he replied quietly. "Now I'm just using those skills to keep our family safe."

Through the window, they watched their children spill out into the yard, their play slightly subdued but still innocent. Austin was visible in his own driveway, telling another neighbor about Daniel's failed truck project and their plans for golf later.

For now, the performance had worked. But Daniel knew they were running out of time before the pretense became impossible to maintain. The truck needed to be ready soon.

Before their neighbors realized just how thoroughly they'd been deceived.

Throughout the morning Daniel worked on the truck inside the closed garage fixing some of the last things and loading it up while Jessica continued to prepare for the trip.

The afternoon sun beat down mercilessly as Daniel lined up his shot, sweat trickling down his back beneath his polo shirt. The sweet spot of his 7-iron connected with the golf ball, sending it arcing across the empty field behind the Peterson place. Dried grass crunched beneath his feet as he stepped back, maintaining his easy smile.

"Nice shot," Austin called out, shadows from gathering clouds dancing across his face. "Your swing's actually improved since last month at the club."

Daniel chuckled, the sound practiced and casual. "Amazing

what a little forced downtime can do for your game." He watched Austin set up his own shot, noting how his neighbor's hands trembled slightly despite his attempt at country club nonchalance.

Across the street, Jessica reclined in a lawn chair, her designer sunglasses hiding watchful eyes as she pretended to read one of her book club selections. Lily and Ryan played a halfhearted game of tag in their front yard, their movements constrained by their mother's insistence they stay close. The whole scene carried a desperate artifice – a Norman Rockwell painting with rot beneath the surface.

"Think we'll get that thunderstorm?" Austin nodded toward the building clouds, his shot going wide. "Might be nice, cool things down a bit."

"Weather's been strange lately," Daniel agreed, thinking of the aurora that still painted the night sky in alien colors. He pulled another ball from his pocket, the familiar motion masking how his eyes constantly scanned their surroundings. Two houses down, Mr. Peterson paced his driveway, phone in hand, still trying to find a signal. The Mitchell kids rode bikes in tight circles, their mother hovering anxiously nearby.

The day dragged on in a parade of manufactured normalcy. Daniel kept one eye on his watch – eighteen hours until their planned departure. In the garage, the old Ford sat nearly ready, just a few final adjustments needed under the cover of darkness. He'd worked on it in careful bursts, always following a show of frustration visible to any watching neighbors.

"You know," Austin said, setting up another shot, "maybe we should organize a neighborhood cookout. Before all this food in our freezers goes bad." His casual tone didn't quite mask the predatory gleam in his eyes. "Pool our resources, make the best of things."

"Could be fun," Daniel replied smoothly, already calculating how to avoid it. "Though Jessica's been cooking everything she can on the gas stove. Making it into a game for the kids – pioneer days, you know?"

A distant explosion made them both turn. Smoke rose from somewhere near the highway, followed by the sharp crack of gunfire. Austin's grip tightened on his club.

"Probably just transformers again," Daniel said quickly. "Like we were hearing yesterday."

"Right." Austin's laugh sounded hollow. "Those repair crews, hard at work."

The afternoon heat pressed down like a physical weight, carrying the acrid scent of distant fires. Daniel found himself categorizing every detail, knowing it might be the last time he saw this place. The perfect landscaping is already showing signs of neglect without automated sprinklers. The Tesla charging stations standing useless in driveways. The façade of civilization growing thinner by the hour.

"Daddy!" Lily's voice carried across the yard. "Can we have popsicles?"

"Sorry, princess," he called back. "They all melted, remember? But Mom's got some special treats planned for dinner."

Jessica raised her book in acknowledgment, her staged serenity masking how she'd spent the morning carefully packing their remaining supplies. They'd hidden bags in the garage rafters, tucked emergency supplies behind boxes, all while maintaining their performance of mild inconvenience.

"Should probably wrap this up," Daniel said, checking his

watch again. "Promised the kids we'd play some board games before dinner. Silver lining to no TV, right?"

Austin nodded, gathering their makeshift driving range. "This was good, Thompson. Normal. We need more normal right now."

Daniel clapped him on the shoulder, the gesture friendly but carefully calculated. "Same time tomorrow? Assuming the power's not back by then."

"Sure," Austin agreed, his smile not quite reaching his eyes. "Tomorrow."

They both knew there would be no tomorrow, but for different reasons. Austin probably planned to organize his "resource pooling" by then. Daniel planned to be halfway to Maine.

The rest of the day unfolded in careful choreography. Jessica prepared dinner on the gas stove, letting the smell of cooking food drift through open windows – a show of normalcy for watching neighbors. The children played board games by battery-operated lantern light, their voices carefully modulated to carry just enough cheer to any listening ears.

As sunset painted the sky in impossible colors, Daniel made a show of checking the Ford's engine again, slamming the hood and kicking the tire in apparent frustration. "Piece of junk," he declared loudly enough for his voice to carry. "Should've stuck to golf."

But his hands, hidden from view, had made the final adjustments. The truck was ready.

As darkness crept in, the neighborhood settled into uneasy quiet. The aurora danced overhead, its ethereal light casting strange shadows across their suburban sanctuary. Through windows, Daniel watched the dim glow of battery-operated lanterns fade one by one as households conserved their precious remaining power. He wound his grandfather's mechanical watch carefully, the familiar motion grounding him in this increasingly alien world.

Five-year-old Lily yawned dramatically from her spot on the couch. "Daddy, will my nightlight work tomorrow?"

"Maybe, Princess," he lied, his heart aching at her innocent question. "We'll see what happens after you get some sleep."

Ryan looked up from his board game, hope still bright in his eyes. "So we're really not going to Grandpa's farm?"

"Not if the power comes back," Jessica answered smoothly, catching Daniel's eye. They'd agreed – let the children sleep tonight believing everything would return to normal. It would make the morning easier.

Jessica began their practiced bedtime routine early. "Since we don't have TV," she announced cheerfully, "we might as well get some extra sleep!"

The children complained as children normally would and the sound carried of Jessica trying to comfort them with promises of some new fun tomorrow if only they'd go to bed.

For now, Daniel maintained his performance. He stepped out for some air and to close the garage. He paused standing in his driveway, sharing a neighborly wave with Austin across the street. "Maybe tomorrow!" he called out cheerfully. "Power's bound to come back soon!"

The lie sat on his tongue like a bitter pill, but his smile never wavered. The time for truth would come with the predawn darkness. Until then, they played their parts in this suburban theater of denial, while under the cover of night, they would make their escape north.

He turned and went back inside, closing and locking the garage door as he did.

Daniel sat motionless in the darkness of his living room, the aurora's ethereal light casting strange shadows through the windows. His grandfather's watch ticked steadily against his wrist, marking each endless minute of his vigil. The neighborhood wasn't as still as it should have been.

A shadow detached itself from the Peterson's garage – Austin, moving with exaggerated stealth. Daniel watched through barely parted curtains as his neighbor emerged carrying what looked like the Peterson's camping gear. Ten minutes later, Austin slipped into the Mitchell's open garage, emerging with their emergency generator.

The scene repeated throughout the night. Austin moved house to house like a suburban raccoon, picking through his neighbors' preparations, amassing supplies in his own garage. Each trip grew bolder, his movements becoming less cautious as his theft went unchallenged.

Around midnight, Austin's shadow fell across Daniel's driveway. Footsteps crunched on gravel, moving toward their garage.

Daniel knocked his hand deliberately against the wall, his voice carrying clearly through the open window: "Damn it, forgot water. Need to head upstairs." He made a show of moving through the house, footsteps heavy on the stairs.

The shadow retreated quickly. Through the upstairs window, Daniel watched Austin hurry back to his own property, garage door closing quietly behind him.

The hours crept by. Daniel wound his watch again, its

steady ticking a counterpoint to his racing thoughts. He mentally rehearsed their route north, each turn and alternative path carefully memorized. The weight of his family's survival pressed against his chest, making each breath feel inadequate.

At 2:45 AM, he moved silently through the house, gently waking Jessica. She came alert instantly, years of motherhood making her naturally quiet. No words were needed – they'd planned this moment carefully.

While Jessica dressed and gathered last-minute items, Daniel crept into the garage. Every movement was measured, calculated. They'd packed the truck's bed strategically – heaviest items secured first, everything cushioned to prevent rattling. Tarps covered their supplies, making the truck appear empty to casual observation.

By 3:15 AM, the truck was ready. Daniel eased back into the house, pausing at the foot of the stairs. This would be the hardest part.

Ryan woke quickly, understanding in his eyes – they'd prepared him for this possibility, disguised as a game. Lily was harder, confused and sleepy. Jessica gathered her up, whispering soothingly, while Daniel helped Ryan with his shoes.

The garage felt cavernous as they gathered beside the truck. Daniel eased the door open manually, thankful for the recent oiling that prevented any squeaks. The pre-dawn air carried a chill despite the summer season.

"Remember," he whispered, "just like we practiced. Mom steers, I push. No doors closing, no talking until we're past the Williams' house."

Jessica slipped behind the wheel, Lily cradled sleepily in her lap. Ryan pressed against her other side, making himself small. The bench seat they'd mocked as outdated now proved perfect – no noisy door for the kids.

Daniel's muscles burned as he pushed against the truck's tailgate. The weight shifted, then began to roll. The slope of their driveway helped, gravity pulling them forward into darkness. Jessica kept the wheel straight, letting them glide silently into the street.

The aurora painted everything in shades of green and purple, making the familiar houses look alien and threatening. Each shadow could be Austin, each rustle of wind could be a neighbor waking. But the truck rolled steadily downhill, picking up speed on the gentle slope of Oakwood Drive.

Daniel jogged beside the driver's window, one hand on the door to guide them. Past the darkened Mitchell house. Past the Peterson place where Austin had stolen camping gear hours earlier. Past the Williams' house that marked the edge of their neighborhood.

The intersection ahead marked the bottom of the hill—and their moment of truth. Once they started the engine, there would be no more pretense, no going back. Daniel's hand found Jessica's in the darkness, squeezing once.

"Ready?" he breathed.

She nodded, shifting to make room as he slipped behind the wheel. The kids remained absolutely silent, understanding the gravity of the moment despite their age. Daniel's hand shook slightly as he turned the key.

The engine caught on the first try, its rumble impossibly loud in the pre-dawn quiet. Daniel engaged the clutch smoothly, decades of muscle memory taking over. They rolled forward into whatever tomorrow might bring, leaving behind their carefully crafted life of denial.

In his rearview mirror, the aurora painted their neighborhood in otherworldly colors. Somewhere in that false dawn, Austin slept surrounded by his neighbors' stolen supplies, dreaming of Daniel's promised golf game that would never come.

The rumble of the engine was louder than normal as it bounced off houses they passed. Inside, some small lights emerged in windows as people inside snapped on lanterns or flashlights. But before any could approach, they were long gone. He drove the truck without lights guided only by the natural light of the auroras making his way for the interstate and north toward what he hoped would be safety.

Beth

Day Two Post CME—Cornish, Maine

CHIEF BETH MARTIN GUIDED HER CROWN VICTORIA into the strip mall's parking lot, the cruiser one of the few pre-1980s vehicles still running in town. The Shop & Save's wide front windows reflected the morning sun, the store's interior dim without its usual fluorescent glow. A handful of cars dotted the lot—mostly older models that had survived whatever had killed their modern counterparts.

She parked near what everyone referred to as Miller's Pharmacy, although technically it was Community Pharmacy. Mr. Miller had been the pharmacist for as long as she could remember. She positioned her car for a clear view of both the liquor store and the grocery store entrances. The feed store at the far end of the strip was already seeing steady foot traffic—everyone suddenly remembering they might need to grow their own food.

"George?" she called out, pushing through the pharmacy's propped-open door. The little bell chimed in the heavy July air. "It's Beth. Just checking in."

George Miller appeared from behind the pharmacy counter, dabbing his forehead with a handkerchief. His white coat looking freshly pressed despite everything—old habits dying hard. "Chief Martin. Twice in one morning? People will talk."

She managed a small smile, remembering her earlier visit to check his security. "Just finishing my rounds. Told James Thompson I'd keep an eye out while they picked up some things for Elena."

George nodded toward where James and Emily stood examining prenatal vitamins. "Everyone's trying to stock up. Can't blame them. Was going to head to the feed store myself after closing, see about some seeds. Marianne's always wanted a garden."

"My mother's medications," Beth started, but George was already reaching under the counter.

"Got them set aside." He slid a small paper bag across. "But Beth… this is the last refill I can manage. Without deliveries…" He left the sentence hanging.

The implications hit her like a physical blow. Her mother's heart condition. No refills. No deliveries. No—

The bell chimed again.

Tommy and Sean Burke stumbled in, the brothers' movements too sharp, too desperate. Beth's hand instinctively moved toward her weapon, but Tommy's gun was already out.

"Nobody move!" Tommy's voice cracked, betraying his youth. Just twenty-three, Beth remembered. Used to help his father with hay deliveries to the Thompson farm. She glanced at James and could see the recognition in his eyes.

"Boys," George said softly, raising his hands. "Let's talk about this."

"Shut up!" Sean moved toward the pharmacy counter, a gym bag clutched in his sweating hands. "We need… we need everything. All of it. The oxy, the—"

"Tommy." Beth kept her voice steady, professional. "Put the gun down. We can figure this out."

Tommy's eyes were wild, pupils blown. Already using, Beth realized. Bad sign. She'd watched their father struggle with pills after the logging accident. Now here were his sons, following the same path.

"You don't understand," he said, the gun wavering between her and George. "You don't... Portland's burning. Everything's falling apart. We need—"

"Protection," Sean finished, vaulting over the counter. "Insurance. Just... just let us take what we need, and nobody gets hurt."

James had pushed Emily behind the feminine hygiene display, his body tense. Beth caught his eye, shaking her head slightly. *Don't be a hero.*

"Boys," George tried again, moving to block the narcotic cabinet. "Your father would—"

The gunshot was deafening in the small space.

George stumbled backward, a look of absolute surprise crossing his face as red bloomed across his white coat. He reached out, seemingly more for balance than anything else, and knocked over a display of vitamins. The bottles clattered to the floor; the sound punctuating their stunned silence.

"No!" Emily broke free from James, her nurse's training taking over. She rushed to where George had collapsed, already pulling gauze from her bag. "No, no, no..."

Tommy stared at his smoking gun as if he'd never seen it before. "I didn't... I didn't mean to..."

Sean was shoving bottles into his bag. Hurried panic with

frantic movements. They clearly did not expect this. "We gotta go. We gotta go now!"

Beth's weapon was in her hand, and she gave chase, but the boys were already running toward the feed store.

Through the open door, she heard their father's old truck roar to life—one of the few vehicles that still ran. Its engine faded into the distance as Emily continued CPR. Strained cries in the distance followed by two more gunshots before the eerie silence returned, leaving only the sound of Emily's desperate attempts to save George.

"Chief." James's voice was tight. "Chief, he's not…"

Beth moved around the counter. George lay still, eyes fixed on nothing, while Emily's hands grew red trying to stem bleeding that had already stopped. The old pharmacist's face looked peaceful, almost surprised, as if he couldn't quite believe what had happened in his own store.

"Emily," Beth said gently. "Emily, he's gone."

"No." Emily's voice broke as she continued compressions. "No, I can still… I can…"

James kneeled beside his daughter, gathering her into his arms. "Honey. Stop. Just… stop."

Beth moved to secure the scene automatically before realizing there was no scene to secure. No crime lab coming. No detectives to call. No system to process the first murder Cornish had seen in decades.

Just an old man's body growing cold on his pharmacy floor, and the knowledge that everything had changed.

She reached for her radio—one of the few still working— to call Jerry at the station. They'd need help to move the body. And George's wife, Marianne, would need to be told. And the narcotics cabinet would need to be secured. And… and…

The sound of shattering glass from the liquor store cut through her thoughts. Then another crash from the Shop & Save. The first real looting in Cornish had begun.

A crowd was gathering in the parking lot, drawn by the gunshot. Some were already moving toward the broken windows, while others stood watching, uncertain. Beth saw Frank Wilson among them, that calculating look in his eyes as he assessed the situation before stepping into the liquor store.

She kneeled beside George, gently closing his eyes. "I'm sorry," she whispered, though whether to George or to the town itself, she wasn't sure.

A wave of stifling air pushed through the open door, carrying the acrid scent of something burning in the distance. Another crisis calling. But for just a moment, Beth remained kneeling beside her old friend, watching the last remnants of their normal world bleed out across his pristine white coat.

The sound of more breaking glass pulled her back to duty. She had choices to make now—try to stop the looting, or focus on securing what remained of the pharmacy's controlled substances. Either way, she knew Cornish would never be the same after this morning.

Six years as a state trooper and three as chief had taught her to read a crowd. The people gathering outside weren't just onlookers anymore. They were waiting to see what she'd do. What rules still applied in this new world.

James seemed to read her thoughts. "Beth," he said, still holding Emily but reaching for her arm. "You can't stop all of them alone."

She nodded, her decision made. "Help me with the

narcotics cabinet. We need to get everything secure before—"

"What about the Walgreens?" Emily asked suddenly, her voice still shaky. "Up the street? They'll have supplies too."

Beth shook her head, gazing at George. "Already gone. Crowd from Steep Falls cleaned them out this morning. Broke both front windows getting in. That is why I've been checking on George every hour or so." She turned to James. "Can you two…?"

"We'll take care of him," James said, his eyes moving along the back counter where the prescription drugs were kept. "And secure what's left here."

Beth nodded, already moving toward the door as more crashes echoed from outside. The Shop & Save's windows were completely shattered now, a stream of people pushing through the broken glass. She recognized most of them—neighbors, friends, people she'd known her whole life, now scrambling like desperate animals.

Her hand found her weapon. One shot into the air, aimed toward the cemetery on the other side of the street. The crack of the gun froze the crowd momentarily, faces turning toward her with expressions ranging from shame to defiance.

"Listen to me—" she started, but movement from the liquor store caught her eye.

Frank Wilson emerged pushing a shopping cart loaded with bottles, his usual morning drink clearly already consumed. He spotted her and changed direction, shoving the cart hard toward the feed store as he broke into a stumbling run.

The crowd erupted. Someone threw a punch. A woman screamed. Two men fought over a case of water while others pushed past them into the store. Curses and threats filled the air as years of small-town civility evaporated in the July heat.

Beth stood frozen, watching people she'd known her entire life tear into each other like animals. Her training felt useless—there was no procedure for watching your whole town dissolve into chaos. Six years as a state trooper had taught her how to handle drunk drivers and domestic disputes. Nothing could have prepared her for this.

She backed up toward the pharmacy, her hands trembling. James met her at the door as she pushed back inside, his expression grim.

"I can't—" The words caught in her throat. She'd tried to maintain order and a professional composure, but the veneer of the false bravado crumbled. Her shoulders slumped as they peered through the doorway, the scene now descending into utter chaos. Mrs. Henderson, who taught her third-grade math, threw a can of soup at Mr. Tucker from the hardware store. The scene straight out of a zombie movie, she spun around saying, "I don't know how to—"

James's hand found her shoulder as the first sob broke free. She turned away from the chaos, ashamed of her tears, but he kept his grip firm. "It's okay," he whispered. "You don't have to carry this alone."

Movement near the broken windows snapped them both to attention. Sherman Masters led a group of men toward the pharmacy, their intentions clear in their rigid postures.

James moved in front of Beth as they closed the door and backed inside. He stood rigid in the entry, producing a .45 from beneath his jacket. The barrel gleamed in the dim light as he leveled it at the approaching group.

"That's far enough, Sherman." James's voice carried clearly despite the noise outside. "You really wanna die for some aspirin?"

Sherman froze, eyes darting between James's unwavering weapon and George's body visible on the floor where Beth kneeled beside it. The men behind him shifted uncomfortably, suddenly unsure.

"James," Sherman started, "we just—"

"You just nothing." James's finger rested steady on the trigger. "Take a good look, Sherman. Is this what we are now? Is this what you want Cornish to become?"

The men shuddered and backed away, the sight of George's blood-stained coat finally driving home the reality of what was happening to their town.

OFFICER JERRY PALMER'S ARRIVAL GAVE BETH THE backup she needed, and time to take care of George's body while speaking to Emily about the prescriptions and medicines Elena needed. James finally lowered the .45, his arm aching from holding it steady. The weight of what had just happened—what he'd been prepared to do to his neighbors—settled in his chest like a stone.

"James." Beth's voice was steady now, professional again despite her earlier breakdown. "Help Emily gather everything."

He shook his head. "We're not looters."

Beth pulled him aside, her voice dropping. "Listen to me. We can't secure these stores. Not anymore. The Grovers are barricading the feed store—smart people, thinking ahead. We'll move what critical supplies we can from the other stores and try to set up a distribution system." She glanced at Emily, who was checking labels on prescription bottles. "Your daughter's a nurse. She knows what people need, how to handle medications properly. And with Elena…"

"Still." James watched Emily methodically filling a duffel bag as Beth had instructed her. "Taking advantage of—"

"This isn't taking advantage." Beth's grip on his arm tightened. "This is survival. And not just for your family.

You're on Pound Hill. Isolated enough to be defensible, central enough to help." She met his eyes. "We're going to need that. Need you."

Emily's voice carried from behind the counter. "Dad, they have prenatal vitamins. And folic acid. Elena needs these." She held up bottles, her hands trembling slightly. "And we need to gather all the antidepressants. People will need to be weaned off properly—cold turkey can cause psychosis, seizures. I don't even want to think about what will happen after today." Emily shuddered, shaking off the chill that she offered them.

"We could store everything at the feed store," James suggested, glancing toward the Grovers' place.

Beth shook her head. "They're protecting their own, sure enough, but…" she said, hesitated and continued, "I'd feel better if our only medical professional has control of the medications. Especially the controlled substances."

James nodded slowly. "We've got that storage room off the barn. Good ventilation, solid door. Could convert it into a temporary pharmacy."

"We'll need people to bring their old prescription bottles," Emily added, already in organization mode. "Without the computer records, it's the only way to verify correct medications and dosages. Cross-reactions can be deadly if we're not careful."

They worked quickly, efficiently. Emily's medical training guiding their choices as they systematically cleared the pharmacy—antibiotics, pain medications, chronic disease management drugs. Beth added a separate pack filled with all the carefully labeled narcotics.

"Keep these secure," she said grimly. "Hidden. They'll be the first things people come looking for when withdrawal hits."

James thought of the Burke brothers, of Tommy's wild eyes. How many others would follow that desperate path? A terrible thought followed. What if they came looking? Would this place his family at risk?

"I'll bring what's salvageable from Walgreens later," Beth continued, interrupting his thoughts. "We'll need to set up some kind of dispensary system. Controlled distribution."

Emily nodded, already making mental notes. "We'll need to inventory everything. Track prescriptions, manage doses. Some medications interact badly—we can't just hand things out randomly." She paused, holding up a bottle of antidepressants. "These are especially critical. Missing even a few doses can trigger severe reactions, as I said before. Panic attacks, paranoia, suicidal thoughts, this is the most crucial thing to consider with so many people now taking them. We are talking about severe psychotic breaks. And with everything else going on…"

"Your mother can help organize," James said, thinking of Sarah's administrative skills. "Set up a record-keeping system. She needs something to focus on."

They loaded everything methodically—first aid supplies, medications, whatever might help them manage the medical needs of a community cut off from modern healthcare. Each item felt both like theft and salvation.

"You know where to find us," James told Beth as they finished loading most of the prescription medications and other things. "Pound Hill. If you need…" He trailed off, unsure how to finish.

Beth nodded, understanding. "Same to you." She glanced back at the pharmacy, at George's sheet-covered form. "Things are changing fast. We need people we can trust."

"I'll be back to help secure the feed store," James assured her. "Once Emily and the supplies are safe at the farm. I'll grab Michael and have him come help."

"First thing is first," Beth said, "you return for the rest of these supplies. I want this store cleaned out... All of it!"

James reluctantly agreed, saying he'd grab the farm truck and let the others unload this one. The second day since the lights went out and people were already losing it. What would happen in the coming weeks, months, even years?

The drive home was silent, each of them lost in thought. The medications in the truck bed represented more than just supplies—they were a responsibility James hadn't asked for but couldn't refuse.

When they crested Pound Hill, James saw Michael already at the gate, rifle ready. Their eyes met as James pulled in, and he knew they'd have hard conversations ahead about security, about community, about what lines they were willing to cross to survive.

But first, they had a pharmacy to build and plans to make. The sun wasn't even at its peak, and already the world had shifted beneath their feet once again.

Maddie

Interstate 95 North - Night Two

THE AURORA PAINTED THE ABANDONED SEMI IN shifting waves of green and purple, its white trailer glowing like a ghost ship on the darkening highway. Maddie's legs burned from hours of pedaling as she propped her bike against the truck's massive wheel. The rubber still held warmth from the day's heat, a strange comfort against her palm.

"Perfect thumbnail backdrop," Grace announced to her dead phone, her voice carrying that same unsettling perkiness. "Urban exploration meets apocalyptic aesthetic. Don't forget to smash that like button!"

Hannah shot Maddie a worried look as she examined the truck's cab. "Door's unlocked. Sleeper compartment looks intact." She rattled the handle. "Could be worse for the night."

"Hashtag vanlife," Grace giggled, swaying slightly. "Hashtag nomad lifestyle. Remember to use my code GRACESURVIVAL for twenty percent off your next--"

"Grace." Maddie kept her voice gentle but firm. "Help me with these bikes. We need to get them hidden before full dark."

The younger girl blinked, her movements jerky as she grabbed her handlebars. "Behind the scenes content! My followers love--" She stopped abruptly, head tilted. "Do you hear that?"

Maddie listened, every muscle tensing. Just crickets and the soft whisper of wind through tall grass along the highway median. "What do you hear, Grace?"

"Notifications." Grace's eyes went wide, unfocused. "So many notifications. My last post must have gone viral! I knew the aesthetic would--"

"Here." Hannah guided Grace toward the truck's steps. "Let's get you settled. I need to check your feet anyway - those blisters looked angry earlier."

The sleeper cab smelled of old coffee and cigarettes, with undertones of something sweeter - air freshener maybe, shaped like a little pine tree and probably long since faded. Maddie helped Hannah hoist Grace into the narrow bunk while searching for any signs of previous occupants.

"Going live from my cozy vanlife setup!" Grace announced to the shadows. "Don't forget to join my Patreon for exclusive behind-the-scenes content of--" She broke off, fingers flying across her blank phone screen. "Oh my god, so many super chats coming in! Thank you xXDarkKnight420Xx for the hundred bits!"

Hannah began unpacking their medical supplies, her movements precise despite the tremor in her hands. "We should try to get some food in her. She barely touched breakfast or lunch."

"Doing a mukbang!" Grace declared, then lowered her voice to a whisper. "ASMR edition. Remember to wear headphones for the full immersive--"

A distant explosion made them all freeze. Through the windshield, an orange glow bloomed on the horizon - another piece of civilization burning itself out. Grace's livestream commentary continued in increasingly fragmented bursts.

"Don't forget to like and subscribe," she mumbled, curling into herself on the bunk. "Ring that bell for notifications… algorithm… hashtag blessed… hashtag…" Her voice cracked. "Hashtag help me."

Maddie climbed into the driver's seat, scanning their surroundings through the big side mirrors. The aurora's light made everything look alien, unreal. Perfect for Grace's deteriorating grip on reality.

"Should we…" Hannah hesitated, sorting through their dwindling supplies. "Should we try to find help? For her? There must be hospitals or…"

"Where?" Maddie asked softly. "Everything's dark. Everything's broken. We just have to get her home." She turned back to watch Grace typing on her dead phone. "Her parents will know what to do."

Grace's voice drifted from the bunk, small and lost: "Don't forget to like and subscribe… please like and subscribe… please… someone… anyone…"

The night pressed against the windows as Hannah divided their remaining food into careful portions. Maddie kept watch, the ghost-light of the aurora reflecting off abandoned cars stretching endlessly north and south. Somewhere ahead lay home - if home still existed. Somewhere behind, Boston burned.

And Grace, huddled in the truck's narrow bunk, whispered to her imaginary audience until exhaustion finally pulled her into uneasy sleep.

Morning crept in with deceptive gentleness, the aurora's ghostly light giving way to harsh sunlight. Grace stirred, her hand automatically reaching for her phone.

"Time to check those notifications," she mumbled, then froze. Her fingers jabbed repeatedly at the black screen. "What… why isn't it…"

"Grace," Maddie started carefully, "maybe the charger--"

"You didn't charge it." Grace's voice dropped to a whisper. Her head snapped up, eyes suddenly wild. "You didn't charge it at all, did you?"

Hannah shifted forward. "The power's still out, Grace. Remember? Nothing works."

"Liar!" Grace clutched the phone to her chest. "You're lying! Maddie, you're just… you're jealous!" Her voice took on a fevered pitch. "You've always been jealous of my following. My brand. My success!"

"That's not--" Maddie reached toward her friend.

Grace exploded off the bunk. "Don't touch me!" She grabbed a fistful of Maddie's hair, yanking hard. "You sabotaged my charger! Trying to silence my voice! My followers need to know the truth about you!"

"Grace!" Hannah tried to separate them as Maddie gasped in pain. Grace's bag swung wildly in the struggle, contents scattering across the cab floor. Prescription bottles clattered under the seats.

Hannah grabbed one, more to keep it from rolling away than anything else. Her medical training made her automatically check the label. "Grace… you're on Clozapine?"

"That's private!" Grace released Maddie's hair, lunging for the bottle. "Give it back!"

Hannah held it out of reach, spotting another bottle. "And Seroquel? Grace, these are…" Her voice trailed off as understanding slowly dawned. "How long have you been taking these?"

"What does it matter?" Grace's voice shifted between her influencer persona and raw panic. "My followers don't need to know about my personal health journey! This isn't part of my brand!"

Maddie rubbed her scalp, watching Grace's increasingly erratic movements. "Grace, when was your last dose?"

"STOP TRYING TO CONTROL MY NARRATIVE!" Grace screamed, holding up her dead phone like a weapon. "I see what this is! You're trying to cancel me! Trying to destroy everything I've built!"

Hannah's face had gone pale as medical knowledge clicked into place. "Grace, honey, these medications... missing doses can cause serious--"

"Going live!" Grace announced suddenly to her blank screen, voice rising hysterically. "Exposed! So-called friends trying to smear my reputation! They're just jealous of my metrics, my engagement rates! Don't let them silence your favorite content creator!"

The realization hit Hannah and Maddie simultaneously; their friend wasn't just scared or stressed. She was in full psychotic break.

The morning sun beat down mercilessly as they followed Grace outside the truck. She paced between abandoned cars, still clutching her dead phone like a talisman, muttering about engagement rates and follower counts.

"Grace," Hannah kept her voice soft, empathy warring with growing fear. "These medications are important. They help you feel balanced, remember?"

"Balanced?" Grace's laugh held a manic edge. "My content doesn't need balancing! My followers love my authentic self!" She jabbed frantically at the black screen. "Tell them! Tell them how authentic I am!"

Maddie took a careful step forward, hands raised. "We're your friends, Grace. We just want to help--"

"Friends?" Grace's eyes snapped to Maddie, something dark and terrifying crossing her face. "Is that what you call someone who sabotages your platform? Who tries to SILENCE YOUR TRUTH?"

Hannah held out one of the pills. "Please, Grace. Just take your medication. We can figure everything else out after--"

"POISON!" Grace screamed, backing away. "They're trying to poison me! Going live with breaking news - my so-called best friend Maddie Foster is an industry plant! Sent to destroy my brand!" Her fingers flew across the dead screen. "Look at these engagement numbers! The algorithm doesn't lie!"

"Grace, please--" Maddie stepped closer.

Grace's face contorted with sudden rage. "Stay back!" She lunged forward, nails raking across Maddie's cheek. "You won't silence me! My followers will know everything!"

"Grace!" Hannah tried to grab her arm, but Grace twisted away with unnatural strength.

"The truth is coming out!" Grace's voice rose to a shriek as she backed away. "Like and subscribe to see Maddie Foster EXPOSED! Watch her whole operation crumble! My followers will--"

She turned and ran, weaving between abandoned vehicles, her voice carrying back in fragments:

"Breaking news! Conspiracy exposed! Don't forget to smash that like button! The truth about Maddie Foster--"

Blood trickled down Maddie's cheek where Grace's nails had caught her. Hannah pressed a gauze pad to the scratches, her hands shaking.

"Three days without antipsychotics," Hannah whispered, watching Grace's figure grow smaller. "God, how did we miss this?"

Grace's voice echoed one last time before she disappeared into the morning haze:

"GOING LIVE WITH THE TRUTH THEY DON'T WANT YOU TO SEE!"

"Grab the essentials," Maddie ordered, throwing supplies into her pack while Hannah gathered the medical kit. "Just what we can carry on two bikes."

Hannah clutched Grace's prescription bottles, hands trembling. "We can't leave her medication--"

"Bring it. But we have to move fast." Maddie slung her pack over her shoulder, wincing as the weight hit her injured arm. "She's heading north. Toward home."

They retrieved their bikes from behind the semi, leaving Grace's propped against the massive tire. The morning sun cast long shadows across the abandoned highway as they pedaled between empty cars, scanning desperately for any sign of their friend.

"She can't have gone far," Hannah called out, but uncertainty crept into her voice. "Not on foot."

They rode in tense silence, the only sound their tires crunching over debris and the occasional distant explosion from the direction of Boston. Grace's social media ramblings had gone quiet - a silence that felt more ominous than her earlier screaming.

The highway rose gradually, giving them a clear view of what lay ahead. Maddie raised her hand in warning as they approached the crest, spotting movement near the bridge.

"Down," she hissed, dragging her bike behind a jackknifed UPS truck. Hannah followed, pressing close to the trailer's sun-heated metal.

The Piscataqua River Bridge stretched before them, its massive structure spanning the water between New Hampshire and Maine. But they found the road onto the bridge blocked. Cars positioned strategically across lanes, armed figures patrolling between them. Even from this distance, they could see weapons glinting in the morning light.

"Looks organized," Hannah whispered. "Not just random looters."

Maddie's heart sank as she scanned the area, seeing no sign of Grace's distinctive strawberry-blonde hair among the figures near the bridge. If she'd made it this far…

"She could have turned off," Hannah suggested, her voice tight with worry. "Maybe she saw them and went another way."

"Or maybe…" Maddie couldn't finish the thought. The scratches on her cheek stung as she squinted into the sun, trying to spot any trace of their friend. "She's not thinking clearly. If she approached them, talking about followers and livestreams…"

Hannah's sharp intake of breath said she understood the implications. They crouched behind the truck, the morning heat already building, faced with an impossible choice—continue searching for Grace, or find another way around the bridge's armed defenders.

Maddie touched the fresh scratches on her cheek, watching another armed figure join the bridge patrol. "If she reached them in that state…"

"We have to keep looking," Hannah insisted, but her voice cracked. "She needs her medication. Without it, she'll just get worse."

A sharp crack echoed from the bridge - a warning shot maybe, or something darker. They both flinched, pressing closer to the truck's hot metal.

"We can't help her if we're dead," Maddie said finally, the words tasting bitter. "There's an exit back there. Down into Portsmouth. We can cut through the city, try to find another crossing."

Hannah clutched Grace's prescription bottles, their rattle too loud in the tense silence. "And if she's still out here somewhere?"

"Then we pray she stayed off the main road." Maddie swung her leg over her bike, keeping low. "We'll work our way up the coast, checking side streets. She has to be somewhere between here and the bridge."

The exit ramp curved past the weathered "Welcome to Portsmouth" sign, depositing them onto empty streets. Abandoned cars cluttered intersections, their doors hanging open as if their occupants had simply evaporated.

"We need a plan," Hannah said, braking beside a knocked-over newspaper stand. "We can't just ride around hoping to spot her."

Maddie scanned the unfamiliar buildings, orientating herself. "First thing - we need a map. Figure out where we are, what bridges we might be able to use."

"There." Hannah pointed toward a Mobil station on the corner. Its windows were broken, but the convenience store portion looked relatively untouched compared to other nearby buildings.

They propped their bikes against the pump island, stepping carefully over broken glass. The store's interior felt oppressively hot, summer heat trapped behind windows plastered with faded advertisements.

"Check the rack by the register," Maddie said, moving toward the counter. "There's usually local maps; tourist guides…Right?"

Hannah rifled through scattered papers while Maddie kept watch through the shattered windows. The street remained quiet except for the occasional distant sound of breaking glass.

"Here." Hannah spread a wrinkled map across the counter. "But Maddie… even with this, how do we find her? She could be anywhere."

Maddie traced possible routes with her finger, trying to think through their options. The scratches on her cheek throbbed, a reminder of Grace's violent confusion. "We need to think like she's thinking. In her mind, she's still broadcasting, still performing. Where would she go for the best 'content'?"

"Assuming she's still…" Hannah stopped, gripping Grace's prescription bottles tighter.

"One problem at a time," Maddie said firmly. "First, the bridges and what is around. She might look for some landmarks to make her posts." Maddie scoffed at the thought of it.

Maddie folded the map and shoved it into her pack as she mounted the bicycle. "Let's head down by the water. There's a park on the map not far away."

They pedaled quickly under the Route 1 bridge deeper into Portsmouth. Along the waterfront and past historic buildings Maddie's eyes scanned every inch of the area. The increasingly narrow streets seemed to close in on them the further into Portsmouth they went. Buildings piled in side by side with no escape between them.

"Up ahead," Hannah said. "Back toward the water. I think it's over that way." She turned left toward another bridge, pedaling slowly up until they could see the water.

Maddie stopped saying, "Let's walk the bikes. We don't wanna get near that bridge too quickly. What if it has people guarding it, too?"

The waterfront park shimmered in the late morning heat, tourist benches lying empty along the harbor walk. Maddie and Hannah had just started to turn away when they heard it - Grace's distinctive "influencer" voice carrying across the abandoned space.

"Welcome to my exclusive behind-the-scenes content!" Grace stood near the water's edge, stripped down to her mismatched underwear, her clothes scattered across the wooden planks. Three men circled her like sharks, playing to her imaginary audience.

"Show them that sexy apocalypse look, baby," one called out, running his hand down her bare arm. Grace giggled, striking poses for her dead phone.

"Oh my god," Hannah whispered, horror creeping into her voice. "We have to--"

"Don't forget to like and subscribe!" Grace twirled, oblivious to the predatory gleam in the men's eyes. One grabbed her waist, pulling her close while another tugged at her bra strap.

"Time for the exclusive content," the third man growled, reaching for her.

Grace's performer's smile faltered. "Wait... the stream is... I need to..." She tried to pull away, reality finally piercing her delusions. "Stop, I don't want--"

"Maddie!" Grace spotted them, her voice climbing with sudden panic. "Hannah! Tell them to stop! Make them--"

Rough hands grabbed her, fingers digging into pale flesh. Grace screamed as one man pressed against her back, another pawing at her chest.

"No!" She twisted violently, breaking free. Without hesitation, she turned and launched herself over the railing. The splash echoed across the harbor as the current caught her immediately.

"GRACE!" Maddie sprinted toward the water's edge, watching her friend surface briefly before the tide yanked her under. Hannah ran alongside, both tracking Grace's head as it bobbed up again, further out now.

"Help!" Grace's cry was weak, already too far away. "I can't—" The current pulled her under again.

She surfaced once more, strawberry-blonde hair plastered dark against her head, arms flailing. Then she went down again. Seconds stretched into eternity as Maddie scanned the water for their friend.

She didn't come back up.

The harbor's dark water swirled empty before her, carrying no trace of Grace's last broadcast. She let out a strained sob beside Hannah, whose tears were already soaking her shirt.

"Oh, Maddie," she choked. "Poor Grace."

"Well, well," a voice drawled behind them. "Looks like we've got two more social media stars."

Maddie turned slowly, feeling the men's shadows fall across her back as they approached, the same predatory look in their eyes.

Daniel

Interstate 95 North—Day Two Post CME

EARLY THAT NEXT MORNING, THE FAMILY QUIETLY slipped from their subdivision and made it to the interstate before sunrise. The on ramp from Andover Street was completely blocked but something caught Daniel's attention drawing him up the street to the used car lot. A massive collection of vehicles lay before them in the predawn hours and an idea formed.

Daniel pulled into the lot with the lights off and waited for a few moments.

"What are we doing here?" Jessica asked.

"Well," Daniel said, glancing at their fuel gauge. "We need fuel."

"How will this place help? None of these cars are going to run." Jessica's face in the dash lights looked troubled.

"I know."

"But—" An understanding of what he planned to do washed over her face, but she didn't say anything more.

He climbed from the truck and gathered a few tools from the bed, making his way to the locked gate. After cutting the lock and opening it, he returned to the truck and pulled around to the side of the building.

"I'll be back," he said, climbing out and pulling the large red gas can from the back.

"Don't you need a hose or something?" Jessica asked.

"I don't plan to siphon it if that is what you mean." He held up a hammer and large screwdriver. "Most of the newer cars have screens in the fill hole and I wouldn't be able to, anyway. I'm going to drain them from the tank itself."

Jessica gasped, "Isn't that dangerous?"

Daniel wasn't sure. He wasn't sure of anything, but he had to try. They wouldn't even make it to the Maine border without fuel.

He skipped the smaller cars with small tanks and went for pickups and bigger SUVs. His goal was to fill the tank and fill the five gallon gas can with spare fuel.

By the time he'd finished, the sun was up. Nervous about being seen, he stowed the last can of fuel and exited the lot. The off ramp from northbound 95 was free from cars and they easily navigated up onto the highway and were now moving toward their family.

It was slow going, weaving among stalled vehicles, and other debris tossed from looted cars and trucks.

The morning crawled by in a series of stops and starts. Daniel's muscles burned from pushing yet another car aside, Ryan trying to help despite his small size while Jessica kept Lily occupied in the truck.

"Almost clear," he called out, sweat soaking through his polo shirt. The July sun beat down mercilessly as they shoved the Prius just far enough to squeeze the Ford through. Ryan beamed with pride at helping, though Daniel noticed his son's hands trembling as they climbed back into the cab.

Near Newburyport, they encountered their biggest obstacle yet - a massive pileup blocking all northbound lanes. Daniel studied it through binoculars from a safe distance, noting movement among the wreckage. He noticed people stripping the cars thinking, *best to avoid them entirely*.

"We'll backtrack to that exit," he told Jessica. "Cross over and use the southbound side."

The detour cost them precious time and fuel, but soon they were heading north again on the wrong side of the highway. The empty southbound lanes felt somehow more eerie than the cluttered northbound side - as if they were driving through an abandoned movie set.

Around eleven, Daniel spotted a shady spot where they could pull over, tucked in next to the trees. "Let's take a break," he suggested, noting how the children had grown quiet and listless in the heat. "Get some food into everyone."

They parked in the shadow of a large oak tree, its leaves providing brief respite from the relentless sun. Jessica distributed water and peanut butter sandwiches while Daniel studied their map, marking their progress.

"How much further, Daddy?" Lily asked between bites, Mr. Trunks propped carefully on her lap to avoid getting peanut butter on his fur.

"We're making good time, Princess." Another lie, but a necessary one. They'd barely covered sixty miles in five hours.

Ryan helped his sister with her juice box, his movements careful, deliberate. The morning's work had aged him somehow - made him more aware of their precarious situation. Daniel caught Jessica's eye, seeing his own worry reflected there.

The rest break stretched longer than planned as the July heat peaked, none of them eager to leave the shade. But eventually, Daniel knew they had to press on. He folded the map carefully, trying to ignore how his hands shook slightly from exhaustion.

"Ready?" he asked his family, receiving tired nods in response.

The Ford's engine growled as Daniel downshifted, threading between abandoned vehicles that materialized after the Merrimack Bridge taking them into New Hampshire. He looked for a place to shift sides again and found a turn around where they were again on the northbound side. His hands ached from gripping the wheel, eyes burning from hours of constant vigilance. In the passenger seat, Jessica maintained her deliberate calm, though her knuckles were white where she gripped the door handle.

"Are we there yet?" Lily's small voice carried from the back seat, where she clutched Mr. Trunks with both arms.

"Soon, Princess," Daniel lied, scanning the road ahead. They'd made decent progress despite the obstacles, but each mile felt like ten with the constant need to navigate through the wreckage of modern civilization.

Movement caught his eye; figures emerging from behind a jackknifed semi. Not just random scavengers this time. These people moved with purpose, spreading across the highway in practiced formation.

"Daniel..." Jessica's voice held a warning.

"I see them." He pressed the accelerator, but they were already surrounded. Men and women in mismatched tactical gear, rifles raised.

A shot cracked against the hood. "Stop the truck!"

Daniel's world narrowed to split-second choices. The gap between two cars. The armed figures converging. The weight of his family's lives in his hands.

He floored it.

Metal screamed as the truck clipped a Honda, sending one attacker sprawling. A woman with a rifle went down, the truck's massive tire rolling over her legs. Her scream cut through the children's terrified cries.

Bullets sparked off metal. The rear window exploded inward, showering them with safety glass. Ryan covered his sister with his body, both children sobbing. Jessica screamed as something punched through the cab near her head.

Then they were through, the engine roaring as Daniel pushed it to its limit. In the rearview mirror, he watched the armed group grow smaller, a few still firing uselessly after them.

"Is everyone okay?" His voice shook. "Jess? Kids?"

Sobbing answers confirmed they were physically unhurt, but the psychological damage was done. Lily's hysteria grew louder, Ryan trying to comfort her between his own broken breaths.

"We're okay," Jessica repeated, more to herself than anyone. "We're okay, we're okay…"

Daniel's adrenaline was just starting to fade when he saw it - the bridge ahead. But not empty like he'd hoped. More armed figures. More blockades. More impossible choices.

"No," he whispered, hitting the brakes hard enough to send them all forward against their seatbelts. The truck skidded to a stop as he stared at the fortified crossing.

Without a word, he threw the truck into reverse, backing up to the exit ramp. The sign read "Portsmouth" in faded green letters. They rolled into the silent city, the sound of their engine unnaturally loud in the empty streets.

Jessica touched his arm, her hand trembling. "Daniel?"

He pulled into an abandoned gas station, letting his head rest against the steering wheel for just a moment. "We'll find another way," he said finally. "We have to."

Behind them, Lily's sobs had quieted to hiccups. Ryan still held her close, his boyish face too old with a fresh understanding of the world they now inhabited. Jessica's breathing slowly steadied, though her hand didn't leave Daniel's arm—anchoring them both to this moment of temporary safety.

The old Ford's engine echoed unnaturally between Portsmouth's historic buildings as Daniel guided them deeper into the unfamiliar city. The narrow colonial-era streets closed in around them, brick walls and wooden storefronts pressing closer with each turn. Their truck—so reassuring on the open highway—now felt exposed, vulnerable.

"The streets are too tight," Jessica whispered, her eyes constantly moving. "If we need to turn around..."

Daniel understood her unspoken fear. The buildings loomed over them, leaving no room for escape. Each intersection presented a new threat—people emerging from doorways, faces appearing in windows, all drawn by the sound of their running engine.

A man stepped into the street ahead, waving his arms. Daniel swerved around him, catching the fury in the stranger's eyes as they passed.

"How?" the man shouted after them. "How is it running?"

More faces appeared. More questions followed. The word spread through the city's strange new grapevine—a working vehicle, moving through their dead streets.

"Daddy?" Lily's voice trembled. "Why are they looking at us like that?"

Ryan pulled his sister closer, both children pressed against the passenger side door. "It's okay," he whispered, though his own voice shook. "Dad won't let anything happen."

The streets grew narrower still as they wound through the historic district. Wooden buildings from the 1700s pressed in on both sides, their windows dark but not empty. Daniel caught glimpses of movement behind glass, shadows tracking their progress.

"We need to find a wider road," Jessica said, her knuckles white where she gripped the door handle. "There are too many places to hide, too many—"

A group of teenagers spilled out of a storefront ahead, pointing and shouting. Daniel's hand tightened on the wheel as he navigated around them, watching in the rearview mirror as they ran after the truck.

"It's working!" one called out. "Hey! Hey, stop!"

"Daniel..." Jessica's voice held a warning as more people emerged, drawn by the commotion.

The truck's engine sound bounced off brick and wood, amplifying in the confined space. Each revolution of the motor announced their presence to anyone within earshot. Daniel felt sweat trickle down his back as he scanned for a way out of the cramped streets.

A woman stepped directly into their path, forcing Daniel to

brake hard. She approached the driver's side, her face desperate. "Please," she called through the glass. "My daughter needs medicine. The hospital in Dover—"

"I'm sorry," Daniel said firmly, but the woman grabbed his side mirror.

"Just tell me how you got it running. Please! We have a car, we just need to know—"

He accelerated carefully, the woman's fingers sliding off the mirror as they pulled away. In the rearview mirror, he watched her sink to her knees in the middle of the street.

"Oh, God," Jessica breathed as they turned onto another narrow road. "Daniel, there are more of them."

People were definitely following now, their pursuit unhurried but deliberate. Some moved parallel to the truck through narrow alleys between buildings, while others trailed openly behind. All of them focused on the impossible sound of their working engine.

"Keep your heads down," Daniel told the children, trying to project confidence he didn't feel. The brick buildings rose like canyon walls on either side, offering too many places for ambush.

A glass bottle shattered against the passenger door, making them all jump. Lily screamed as Jessica pulled both children closer to her.

"They're getting angry," Ryan observed, his young voice tight with fear.

Daniel spotted a promising street ahead—slightly wider, leading toward what looked like the waterfront. But as he turned onto it, his heart sank. More people were gathering, drawn by the sound of their engine and the growing commotion.

"We're being herded," he realized aloud, seeing figures moving to block side streets ahead of them.

"Daniel?" Jessica's voice cracked slightly. "What do we do?"

He checked their fuel gauge—still half full, thanks to their earlier scavenging. But fuel wouldn't help if they got boxed in on these narrow streets. Already their followers had grown to dozens, their pace quickening as they sensed the truck's increasing vulnerability.

Another bottle crashed against the tailgate. Someone shouted about "rich people" and "working cars" and "not fair." The crowd's mood was shifting dangerously.

"Hold on," Daniel said, downshifting as he spotted a gap between buildings. He turned hard, the truck's tires scraping against the curb as they barely cleared the corner.

They emerged onto what appeared to be some kind of waterfront avenue, the street finally opening up. Daniel felt a moment of relief at the wider space—until he saw what waited ahead.

Three men surrounded two young women near the water. The women backing away in a defensive posture. Even from this distance, Daniel could see the predatory intent in the men's stalking movement.

Behind them, their pursuers were still coming but he'd left them in the burst of speed, shooting to this point.

Daniel heard the man, his voice laced with intent. "Looks like we've got two more social media stars," the man called out to his companions. One of the men looked up at the sound of their engine, a cruel smile spreading across his face as he eyed the two women.

Daniel threw the truck into park, every protective instinct firing at once. He caught Jessica's eye, saw understanding flash across her face as she shoved the children onto the floor in the back seat.

"Can I help you gentlemen?" Daniel called out, his voice carrying clearly across the suddenly silent street.

James

Day Three—Cornish, Maine

"WE NEED SOME MORE FEED FOR THE CHICKENS," Michael said, reaching for another biscuit. "And the generator's burning through fuel faster than we expected. If we're going to keep the water running, we have to come up with something else."

James nodded, taking a moment to appreciate his family gathered around the breakfast table. Emily's children, Sophia and Ethan, were busy arranging their eggs into faces on their plates while Elena picked at her toast, Matthew hovering beside her.

"Maybe we could teach the chickens to find their own food," Ethan suggested seriously. "Like in that movie where the animals learn to take care of themselves."

Sophia rolled her eyes at her little brother. "That was a cartoon, dummy."

"Actually," Emily started, a small smile forming, "that's not a bad idea. We could let them free range more, supplement what feed we have."

"Out of the mouths of babes," Michael said, ruffling Ethan's hair.

Sarah emerged from the kitchen with more coffee, the pot scraping slightly as she set it down. "Well, when Daniel gets here, he can help with the chickens. Lily loves animals, and Ryan's old enough to help with chores." She began gathering empty plates. "We'll need to air out the guest room. I changed the sheets, but it still feels stuffy. This damn heat, I swear there hasn't been so much as a slight breeze these past few days."

James caught Emily's eye across the table. "Sarah, honey—"

"Don't." Sarah's voice took on an edge. "Don't you dare tell me they're not coming. We've always agreed that in any emergency, big or small, the farm is where we'd all come." The dishes clattered as she stacked them with more force than necessary. "He will come."

"Mom—" Matthew started, but Sarah cut him off.

"He will come," she repeated firmly. "Now, I need to inventory the pantry like we discussed yesterday. Elena, dear, you should rest. Emily, could you check her blood pressure again?"

Without waiting for a response, Sarah disappeared into the kitchen. The sound of running water momentarily reminded James of the fuel issue but also couldn't quite mask her sharp movements with the dishes.

"I'll help her," James said quietly, standing.

"Dad." Emily's voice stopped him. "Let her be for a minute."

He waved her concern away with a nod. "I know, don't worry."

James found Sarah at the sink, her hands gripping the edge of the counter. "I'm sorry," he said, placing a hand on the small of her back.

She didn't turn around. "Don't be sorry. Be ready. They'll need clean towels, and—" Her voice caught. "Just… be ready."

The moment broke as Ethan's voice carried from the dining room: "Can I name the chickens if they're gonna be our friends now?"

A surprised laugh escaped Sarah. She wiped her eyes quickly, squaring her shoulders. "That boy," she said, her voice steadying. "Just like his mother at that age."

"Sarah—"

"I know what you're thinking," she said, finally turning to face him. "I'm not fooling myself. I know things are… different and going to get hard. But Daniel knows where we are. He knows this is where they'll be safe." She touched James's arm briefly. "Now, we all have work to do."

The family began dispersing to their tasks. Sarah pulled out her notepad, already making lists, while Emily led Elena upstairs for her check-up.

"Dad?" Matthew hovered uncertainly by the stairs. "Should I—"

"Come on," Michael interrupted, clapping Matthew's shoulder. "Barn needs mucking out."

James caught the beginning of Michael's quiet words as they headed outside: "You know, when Emily was pregnant with Sophia…"

Their voices faded, leaving him standing in the suddenly quiet kitchen, watching his wife meticulously write down everything they'd need to handle for a family that might never arrive.

"C'mon Sarah," he said, "Emily needs help in our new barn

pharmacy."

Sarah smiled at him warmly and gripped the crook in his arm that he instinctively bent to hold on to her hand with his other one as they headed out the door.

James steadied the old cabinet like Emily directed him, maneuvering it into its placement along the barn's back wall. The storage room smelled of fresh sawdust and leather, their morning work transforming the space into something resembling a makeshift pharmacy. Sarah stood nearby, clipboard in hand, already organizing medications into categories.

"A little to the left," Emily instructed. "We need space for the antibiotics on that side." She paused, wiping sweat from her forehead. "And the controlled substances should be kept separate, maybe in that locked tack box?"

"The one Grandpa used for his good whiskey?" Sarah asked, a hint of humor in her voice. "Seems fitting."

The crunch of tires on gravel drew their attention. James moved to the barn door, tension settling in his shoulders as he recognized Beth Martin's cruiser pulling up the drive.

"I'll check it out," he said, opening the door

"Emily?" Beth called out, stepping from the car and hurrying to the other side where another officer James remembered from the pharmacy opened the passenger door. He reached into the back seat helping an elderly woman emerge. Even from this distance, James recognized Marianne Miller's silver hair and careful movements.

"Mrs. Miller?" Emily hurried forward, taking over. "Are you alright?"

Marianne's usual dignified bearing seemed somehow

smaller in the morning light. "I'm sorry to intrude," she began, her voice wavering slightly. "But after George…" She stopped, pressing her lips together.

"Come inside," Sarah said firmly, clipboard forgotten. "You must be exhausted. When's the last time you ate?"

Beth caught James's eye as Sarah led Marianne toward the house. "Got a minute?"

James nodded, noting the tension in Beth's stance. They moved away from the others, voices dropping.

"Frank Wilson's been making noise down at the Towne Tavern," Beth whispered. "Lots of talk about 'fair distribution' and 'community resources.' He's three sheets to the wind, but he's drawing a crowd."

"Already?" James ran a hand through his hair. "It's only been a couple of days."

"Times like these…" Beth glanced toward the house where they could see Sarah settling Marianne at the kitchen table through the window. "People show who they really are pretty quick. Look, I know this is a lot to ask, but Marianne can't stay alone. Not with things the way they are, and after George…"

"Of course she'll stay," James said. "Sarah's probably already planning where to put her."

Beth's shoulders relaxed slightly. "Thank you. And James? You might want to think about security up here. Emily's medical knowledge and the drugs… it's going to become more valuable every day."

The weight of that statement hung between them as Beth returned to her cruiser, Jerry already radioing something about a disturbance near the feed store.

Beth opened the cruiser door and paused. "I'm sorry,

James, for bringing so much to your family," she gulped, looking toward the house. "Putting them in danger."

"We'll handle it as it comes. We have to take care of one another," he said.

James remained for a moment where the car had been, watching them drive away, the morning sun suddenly feeling less warm against his skin.

Inside the house, he could hear Sarah's voice: "Now, let's get you settled. I just changed the sheets in the blue room…"

James lingered for a few moments before walking across the yard toward the barn. He could still hear Sarah's voice chatting with Marianne through the open windows over the crunch of gravel as he approached the doorway into the barn. He hesitated, watching Michael guide Matthew toward the far stalls. His steady voice carried across the space as they walked. Michael tried to be less the brother-in-law and more the friend in his stance as he spoke to Matthew.

"You're not helping her, you know." Michael's words were gentle but firm. "Hovering like that, tracking every breath she takes."

"But the baby—" Matthew started.

"Will come when it comes. Right now, you're just adding to her stress. Em says it is actually making it worse. You've got to get it together." Michael handed Matthew a pitchfork. "Here. Manual labor's good for clearing the head."

James moved away before hearing Matthew's response, recognizing the importance of letting that conversation happen without an audience. He busied himself with the morning's tasks, the familiar rhythm of farm work and the children chasing the now free-range chickens almost making things feel normal.

By early afternoon, James found Matthew looking more settled, if exhausted, from whatever Michael had put him through in the barn.

"Wanna take a ride over to Jenkins' with me?" James asked, catching his son wiping sweat from his forehead. "See if he's picked up any news?"

"Sure," Matthew said. "Let me grab a drink."

"Oh, no you don't," Sarah said, walking toward them. "Lunch is ready."

"We need…"

She cut him off. "We need to eat. It'll wait for half an hour while you two clean up and grab a bite. It's all on the counter."

"Yes, Ma'am," James said, smacking Sarah's ass as he walked by.

Matthew, on James' heels, snickered and Sarah eyed them both with a hint of humor in her glance.

They headed out after lunch, the old truck's engine sounded too loud in the heavy summer air as they drove. Matthew stared out the window, his earlier anxiety evident in his restless fingers.

"You know," James said carefully, "when your mother was pregnant with Emily, I nearly drove the doctors crazy." He chuckled at the memory. "Had them checking every little thing. Called them over nothing. Your grandfather finally took me fishing just to get me out of your mother's hair."

Matthew turned from the window. "Really? You?"

"Oh yeah. I was convinced something would go wrong if I wasn't watching every second." James navigated around an abandoned car. "Want to know what actually helped?"

"What?"

"Working the farm. Letting nature take its course." He glanced at his son. "Babies have been coming into this world a lot longer than we've had hospitals and monitors. Elena's strong, and Emily knows what she's doing."

"But with everything that's happened—"

"Makes it scarier, sure." James nodded. "But it doesn't change the basic truth. That baby's coming whether the power's on or not. Question is, what kind of help are you going to be to Elena when it does?"

James hoped he'd helped as his son rode silently beside him, watching the trees go by while they made their way down the road toward Jenkins' place

They pulled into Jenkins' drive, the old man's array of antennas stark against the afternoon sky. But before they could hop out of the truck, Jenkins burst through his front door, face pale beneath his usual wild-eyed expression.

"Thompson! Thank God. You need to hear this." He waved them toward his radio room. "Been picking up transmissions about Seabrook. I never considered the issues from the nuclear plants not being shut down. I fear this is not good."

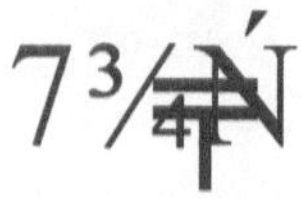

The Feed Store—Cornish, Maine

"You know what I miss most?" Jerry asked, drumming his fingers on the cruiser's dashboard. "Those maple bars from the bakery. Been thinking about them all morning. I'd go get me some and a cup of joe each morning. Ain't been open since the day."

Beth smiled, navigating the Crown Vic around another abandoned car. The July heat was already building, making the vinyl seats sticky despite the early hour. "For me it is my morning routine. Spent the past few years stopping at Pete's Auto on my way to work, shooting the breeze while he made a pretense of checking my oil."

"Pete's a good guy," Jerry said, smirking at her. "I think he's sweet on you."

Beth pretended she didn't hear him but agreed, thinking she might just have to stop on over this morning after they checked out whatever was happening at the feed store.

"At least we've got something," Jerry said. "My Linda's been rationing our food like we're in the Depression. She's got this whole system set up with rainwater and a washboard." He chuckled. "Been lecturing me about conserving everything, though heaven knows we've got enough supplies at home. Says her grandmother taught her all about stretching supplies and doing things the old fashioned way." He shook his head. "Never thought those old stories would matter."

"Your Linda's smart." Beth downshifted as they

approached the intersection, habit making her tap the brake though they hadn't seen another moving vehicle all morning. "We should talk to her about helping to organize a community storage system, maybe even getting others together to share skills. People are getting scared about food and worried that the power isn't coming back."

"Getting scared?" Jerry snorted. "Half the town's already panicked. You saw what happened at the pharmacy." He fell silent, both of them remembering George Miller's blood on the floor.

"People need a sense of normalcy," Beth said, her tone almost forlorn.

"Speaking of 'normal'," Jerry gestured at the row of buildings ahead. "Remember when our biggest problem was breaking up teenage loitering at the feed store?"

Beth's hand gripped the wheel. "That's why we need to get organized. Fast. Before people like Frank Wilson start stirring up more trouble."

"Speaking of trouble… That's a lot of hardware for feed shopping," Jerry muttered, nodding toward the rifles visible in several truck beds.

A cluster of unfamiliar trucks sat outside the feed store. Something about their arrangement tickled her police instincts - not random parking but deliberately positioned. Like a perimeter.

"Is that Sherman Masters?" Jerry asked, pointing toward a figure moving between the vehicles.

Beth reached for the siren switch, intending a quick burst to announce their presence officially. *bwip bwip Weewoo,* the siren sounded and was immediately followed by the sharp crack of gunfire that cut through the morning air as bullets whizzed by, pinging off of abandoned vehicles. The cruiser's hood erupted in a spray of metal as bullets struck home. Steam hissed from the radiator as Beth slammed the car into reverse.

"Down!" she shouted, more shots pinging off the frame as they backed behind an abandoned delivery truck.

Jerry drew his weapon, face grim. "Well, Chief, just like those old Westerns you love to watch."

"Except I don't remember John Wayne dealing with automatic weapons," Beth muttered, assessing their situation. The cruiser was dying, steam now pouring from under the hood. They were pinned down, and their only potential cover lay in the feed store itself - where more shots rang out as the defenders returned fire.

Her breath came in controlled bursts as Beth counted the positions she could see. Three... no, four trucks arranged in a loose arc around the feed store's front entrance. More vehicles behind, partially hidden by the building's bulk. The morning sun caught on rifle barrels, making them glint like deadly stars.

"I count at least eight shooters," Jerry whispered, peering around the delivery truck's bumper. "Plus whatever backup they've got we can't see."

"And Sherman," Beth added grimly. The betrayal stung, though she'd seen enough in the past few days to know loyalty meant little when people got desperate. "Question is, who's he thrown in with?"

Another burst of gunfire erupted from the feed store - defensive positions, Beth noted. The Grovers were in there, had to be. They'd been fortifying the place since day one.

"Radiator's shot," Jerry reported, glancing at their

steaming cruiser. "We're not driving out of here."

Beth keyed her radio, knowing it was probably useless but needing to try. "This is Chief Martin. Sherman Masters, I know you can hear me. Let's talk this through before--"

The response came in another hail of bullets, forcing them both flat against the pavement. Concrete chips stung Beth's cheek as rounds sparked off the delivery truck.

"Think that's a 'no' on negotiations," Jerry muttered.

Movement caught Beth's eye - a flash of color near the feed store's loading dock. Someone inside was trying to signal them. She squinted, making out a familiar face in a narrow window.

"Mike Grover," she breathed. "They're pinned inside, but looks like they've got the high ground." She studied the space between their position and the loading dock. About thirty yards, maybe forty. Exposed except for...

"Jerry, see that dumpster? Then the stack of pallets?"

He nodded, already reading her mind. "Leapfrog cover. Like that training course in Augusta." His grin was tight but genuine. "Though they weren't using live rounds there."

"One more thing." Beth checked her ammunition, mind racing. "Those aren't local weapons. Too new, too military. Portland gang maybe, moving north like we heard."

"Hell of a time for Sherman to pick new friends."

A voice boomed across the parking lot, deep and unfamiliar, "Last chance, Grover! Open up or we burn you out! Plenty more where we came from!"

Beth met Jerry's eyes. "Ready to crash their party?"

"After you, Chief."

They tensed, preparing to move. Beth offered up a silent

prayer, then nodded once.

"Three… two… one…"

The first sprint felt like slow motion. Beth's boots scraped concrete as she dove behind the dumpster, the metallic clang of bullets hitting its side echoing through her bones. Jerry landed hard beside her, breathing heavily.

"Getting too old for this," he gasped.

"Moving!" Beth didn't wait for a response, already pushing off toward the pallets. More shots, but less accurate now - the angle from the trucks forcing their attackers to expose themselves to the feed store's defenders.

She heard Jerry behind her, his rhythmic counting between breaths - a habit from his days running track in high school. The pallets offered sparse cover, bullets splintering wood inches from her head.

That's when she saw it - a gap in the shooting pattern. Amateur move, these Portland boys. Local hunters would know better.

"They're reloading! Now!"

They broke cover together, racing for the loading dock. The concrete expanse felt endless, every step an eternity. Beth's lungs burned as she pushed harder, hearing Jerry's footsteps…

Until they stopped.

The sound of him hitting the ground turned her world red. She spun, weapon drawn, seeing Jerry clutching his leg. Blood already soaking his uniform.

"Go!" he shouted, trying to drag himself toward cover.

Instead, Beth ran back. More shots cracked around them as she grabbed his belt, hauling him forward. Her muscles screamed as she dragged him the last few yards.

The loading dock door burst open. Mike Grover and his son Tommy provided covering fire while rough hands pulled them inside. The heavy door slammed shut behind them, plunging everything into relative darkness.

"Holy shit," someone whispered. Beth blinked, letting her eyes adjust. Jerry lay propped against a feed pallet, face grey with pain. Blood pulsed steadily from his thigh.

"Need a belt," Beth ordered, already shrugging off her uniform shirt. "Something to tourniquet with."

Tommy Grover yanked off his own belt, hands shaking as he passed it over. Beth worked quickly, wrapping her shirt around Jerry's leg first, then using the belt to pull it tight above the wound.

"Some welcome party," Jerry managed through clenched teeth.

"Shut up and stay still." Beth checked his pulse - rapid but steady. The bleeding had slowed, but his pant leg was soaked crimson.

Mike Grover crouched beside them, rifle still trained on the door. "They showed up at dawn. Sherman was with them - said something about 'new management' and 'fair distribution.' When we told them to pound sand…" He shook his head. "Been like this ever since."

A fresh barrage hit the building's metal siding, making them all duck instinctively.

"How many inside?" Beth asked, still monitoring Jerry's pulse.

"Eight of us. Four rifles, couple of shotguns. Been making our shots count, but they've got us surrounded. And they've got…" Mike's voice dropped. "They've got some heavy hardware, Beth. Military stuff. More vehicles coming too, heard them on their radios."

Jerry's eyes fluttered, his skin clammy under Beth's fingers. The tourniquet would buy time, but he needed real medical attention. Soon.

"Chief?" Tommy's voice shook slightly. "What are we gonna do?"

Before she could answer, an engine roared outside - much closer than before. Then another. And another.

Jerry's eyes flickered open at the sound. "That's Pete's old Dodge," he mumbled. "Know that death rattle anywhere."

More engines joined the first - the deep growl of James Thompson's pickup, the steady chug of a farm tractor, and the distinctive purr of what could only be Jenkins' ancient Cadillac.

Mike Grover crouched at the high window, rifle ready. "Got vehicles coming in from the north. Pete's leading them in."

The Portland gang opened fire first, their automatic weapons spraying wildly toward the new threat. Return fire cracked from multiple directions - precise shots from experienced hunters. Two of the gang members went down immediately, their screams cutting through the morning air.

"Get the trucks started!" someone shouted - one of the Portland leaders, Beth guessed. "Move, move, move!"

Engines roared as the gang scrambled for their vehicles. Another exchange of gunfire, more focused now, pinning everyone down. Beth heard the distinctive sound of tires spinning on gravel, then accelerating hard. Through the window, she watched several trucks peel out through a gap between buildings, leaving behind a small box truck and what looked like a Chevy sedan.

"They're running!" Tommy called out.

"Let them go," Beth ordered, still monitoring Jerry's pulse. "We've got wounded to tend to."

The sound of the gang's retreating vehicles faded, replaced by the steady idle of Pete's Dodge and Jenkins' Cadillac. James Thompson's voice carried clearly now: "Beth? Mike? Everyone alright in there?"

"Jerry's hit," Beth called back. "Need medical, fast!"

She caught Mike Grover's eye, both of them knowing this wasn't over.

The door slammed wide, with James and Pete rushing in.

"Quickly, we need to get him up to Emily." Beth's voice faltered and cracked.

"We got this," James said, lacing his arms under Jerry's while Pete gripped his legs and they hoisted him up. "You secure this place and check those vehicles. I'll be back once we get Jerry up to Em."

Beth nodded without words, grateful for their arrival and turned to Mike. "Let's secure the perimeter and check everything."

Maddie

Portsmouth Waterfront—Day Three

DESPITE THE JULY HEAT, AN UNEASY CHILL RAN down Maddie's spine. Grace's final scream echoed in fragments through her mind – mixing with the gentle lap of harbor water against wooden pylons, the splash that had swallowed her friend whole.

"Come here, sweetheart," one of the men called, his words dripping with cruel intent. "Show us some of those social media moves."

She faintly recalled the sound of an old engine cutting through their taunts. A battered truck appeared at the end of the street, its driver emerging with what looked like a tire iron. Despite his expensive polo shirt and neat haircut, something dangerous flashed in his eyes.

"Get the truck!" The shout carried from several blocks away. "Don't let them get away!"

The mob's voices grew louder, bouncing off brick buildings: "Rich bastards with their working cars!" "Grab the girls, too!" "Tear it apart!"

One of the men lunged toward Hannah. The truck driver swung hard, the crack of metal against bone cutting through the chaos. "Come on, tough guy," he growled at the other two. "Try it."

"I'll fuck you up, pretty boy," the larger man snarled, pulling something that glinted in the sun. He tossed it to his other hand and back. Maggie could see it. It looked like a hunting knife, obviously new and unused. He stuck it out, pointing at the man who'd come to their rescue and swirling his hand in a circle, the shimmer of the blade catching her eye again. "Think you're better than us with your fancy truck?"

A woman's voice jerked her attention back to the truck when it pierced through the growing roar of the mob: "They're coming from Cedar Street too!"

Footsteps thundered closer. Dozens of them. Hundreds maybe. The sound of breaking glass and distant screams created a terrible symphony.

An explosion rocked the waterfront, the shock wave hitting Maddie's chest like a physical blow. Heat washed over them as smoke billowed from a building a block away. The acrid smell of burning plastic filled her lungs.

"Get in!" the woman screamed, yanking open the passenger door and waving frantically at them. Maddie focused on the two children huddled in the back seat, a little boy clutching his sister close. "Hurry!"

Hannah's hand found Maddie's arm, squeezing hard. "Maddie, we have to—"

"There's the truck!" Someone emerged from the smoke. "Don't let them—"

Another explosion, closer this time. Through the chaos, Maddie saw the driver swing again, keeping the men back. Blood ran down his arm where the man with the knife had caught him.

The choice crystallized in a heartbeat: certain death here, or trust these strangers. The harbor's dark water still held Grace. They couldn't lose each other, too.

They ran. The woman practically heaved them into the cab slamming the door shut as more people flooded the street. Maddie and Hannah scrambled to get upright in the back seat behind the passenger side, while the children huddled on the floor behind their father, wide eyes riddled with fear, a stuffed elephant clutched between them like a talisman to ward off evil.

"Kill that rich prick!" "Tear them apart!" "Get the fucking truck!"

The driver dove in, blood dripping onto his khakis. The engine roared as he threw it into reverse and stomped on the gas. Something—a brick maybe—shattered against the hood. The woman grabbed his arm as he shifted gears, yelling, "The bridge! Go!"

They shot forward, the truck's engine screaming in protest. Hands reached for them through open windows tearing at Maddie's tank top, ripping apart the shoulder strap. Faces twisted with desperation and rage pressed against the glass on the other side. Hannah lunged to hit the lock button while the children shrieked in fear. She choked and gagged on the stink of unwashed bodies and fear that filled the cab while she struggled to crank the window handle up to block them out.

"Daddy?" The little girl's voice shook. "I'm scared."

"Close your eyes, Princess," he said through gritted teeth, yanking the wheel hard.

They hit the bridge at speed, Portsmouth dissolving into chaos behind them. Hannah's tears soaked into Maddie's shoulder as the harbor disappeared from view, taking Grace with it. The mob's roars faded, replaced by six people breathing too fast in the confined space and the truck's steady growl.

No one said anything until they'd reached the traffic circle and raced up the on ramp back onto the interstate.

"Everyone okay?" the driver asked, blood streaming down his arm and dripping onto the seat. His wife—she had to be his wife—reached toward him, but Hannah was already moving, pulling the small med kit from her pack.

"Let me," she said, pulling supplies from her small kit. "I'm a medical student." The man winced, uneasy, and she explained, "I've been an EMT in South Portland for the past five years." His head dipped and the woman pulled away to let her look at it. Her hands moved with practiced efficiency, cleaning and bandaging the wound even as the truck swerved around abandoned cars. The driver grunted his thanks, keeping his eyes on the road while Hannah worked.

Maddie caught Hannah's eye. Her mind still revolving around the man's words asking if they were okay. Okay? They'd just watched Grace die. Fled in a stranger's truck. Left everything behind. But they were alive. For now.

The little boy shifted beside them, sitting on the seat and pulling his sister up with him. The elephant clutched in his hands now. He studied them with solemn eyes, far too old for his young face. "Did the bad people hurt you, too?"

Hannah's hand found Maddie's, squeezing hard enough to hurt. What could they say? How could they explain what had ended in that harbor? The life of a friend? Hope for a future? Nothing would ever be the same.

The truck wound north, away from whatever remained of their civilization plummeting into the blackness of chaos. Behind them, smoke rose from Portsmouth in thick black columns. And somewhere in that dark water, Grace's final broadcast played to an audience of none.

The truck wound through the maze of abandoned vehicles on I-95, Daniel expertly navigating the clearest paths. Ryan and Lily sat huddled together in the back seat beside Hannah and Maddie, their eyes wide as they watched unfamiliar landscapes roll past.

Hannah finished securing the bandage on Daniel's arm, her hands steadier than her voice. "That should hold, but we'll need to watch for infection."

"Thank you," he said, flexing his arm carefully. "I'm Daniel, by the way. Daniel Thompson." He gestured toward his wife. "This is Jessica, and our children Ryan and Lily."

Lily clutched her stuffed elephant closer, while Ryan maintained his protective posture beside his sister, though his eyes studied Maddie and Hannah with undisguised curiosity.

"Thompson?" Maddie sat forward, heart suddenly racing for a different reason. "From Maine?"

"Cornish," he confirmed. "Though we've been living in Lynnfield, outside Boston. Heading to my father's farm on Pound Hill."

"I'm Maddie Foster. David Foster's daughter? From Cornish? The hardware store?" The words tumbled out in a rush. "Have you heard anything about what's happening there? About my family?"

Daniel's eyes met hers in the rearview mirror, understanding and regret mixing in his expression. "I'm sorry, we've been cut off since this started. Haven't heard anything from up north."

"Grace," Hannah whispered suddenly, her voice cracking. She gripped Maddie's hand tighter.

"Grace?" Jessica turned in her seat, maternal concern crossing her face. "Was there someone else with you?"

Maddie felt tears burning again. "She…" The harbor's dark water flashed through her mind. "We couldn't…" She pressed her face into Hannah's shoulder, shoulders shaking with silent sobs.

Jessica's face softened with realization and deep compassion. "Oh, honey. I'm so sorry."

"Mom?" Ryan's voice came small and worried. "Are they crying because of the bad men?"

"Shh," Jessica soothed, reaching back to touch his knee. "Everyone's safe now."

"I'm Hannah Mitchell," Hannah added quietly, her arm around Maddie. "From Portland. We were touring Harvard when everything happened."

"The farm will be safe," Daniel said firmly, his tone leaving no room for argument. "My father's place has weathered hard times before."

Maddie lifted her head, wiping her eyes. "You really think my family might head there? Dad and your father must know each other, with the hardware store being right in town…"

"It's possible," Daniel said carefully. "Right now, let's focus on getting there ourselves. Still got a long drive ahead."

"But My family is in Portland. I need to go to Portland," Hannah said, the words tumbling out in a stream of near panic.

"We'll try and find them if we can," Daniel said, shifting his tone as he glanced in the rearview mirror again. "I can't put my family in danger again," he cautioned her, "but we will try."

"I understand," Hannah replied, giving Maddie's arm a squeeze.

The truck rumbled steadily north, each mile bringing them closer to whatever remained of their world. Lily had dozed off against her brother's shoulder, her elephant tucked securely under one arm. Ryan's eyes were heavy too, though he fought to stay alert, clearly feeling responsible for his sister.

Maddie studied the passing landscape, trying to recognize anything familiar in the sea of abandoned vehicles. "How much farther is it to Portland?" she couldn't help asking.

"If the roads stay passable and our speed can be maintained?" Daniel checked his mirrors constantly as he drove. "Maybe a couple hours. But we've already seen how quickly things can change."

The sun hung low in the sky as Daniel guided the truck off the highway just past the York toll plaza, finding shade beneath a cluster of maples. They hadn't seen another moving vehicle since Portsmouth, though abandoned cars littered the interstate like fallen leaves.

"Everyone must be hungry," Jessica said, already reaching for their supplies. "Daniel, help me with the tailgate?"

Maddie watched Daniel scan their surroundings before nodding, his movements still tense despite the empty highway. The children tumbled out after their mother, Ryan keeping close to Lily as she clutched Mr. Trunks.

Jessica worked efficiently, spreading packages on the tailgate while Hannah checked Daniel's bandage. The evening air felt heavy with July heat, but somehow cleaner than Portsmouth's smoke-filled chaos.

"Mom packed peanut butter," Ryan announced, helping his sister onto the truck's bumper. "And those good crackers!"

"The ones with the little fishes?" Lily perked up for the first time since Portsmouth.

"Here." Jessica handed out paper plates, her movements practiced. "We need to eat while we can."

Maddie accepted a sandwich, realizing suddenly how hungry she was. When had they last eaten? The morning's protein bars from Martha felt like a lifetime ago.

"So," Jessica said carefully, helping Lily with her juice box, "you girls were touring Harvard?"

Hannah nodded, swallowing hard. "I was accepted to the medical school. Maddie was showing me around since she's at BU and…" Her voice caught.

"I'm sure they'll sort everything out," Jessica said quickly. "Once things get back to normal—"

"Will they?" The question escaped before Maddie could stop it. "Get back to normal?"

Daniel's eyes never stopped moving, scanning the tree line, the highway, the growing shadows. "Different normal, maybe," he said finally. "But people adapt. Survive."

"Like pioneers!" Ryan declared through a mouthful of crackers. "We learned about them in school. They didn't have electricity either."

"That's right, buddy." Jessica smoothed his hair. "And they figured things out."

Lily tugged at Hannah's sleeve. "Are you gonna be a doctor like on TV?"

"That was the plan." Hannah managed a small smile. "Emergency medicine. Though I guess I'm getting more hands-on experience than expected." She gestured to Daniel's bandaged arm.

"You're very good at it," Jessica said warmly. "We're

lucky you were there."

The conversation lulled as they ate, highway winds rustling through maple leaves overhead. For just a moment, it felt almost normal – a family picnic on a summer evening. But the abandoned cars stretched endlessly north and south, and Grace's absence felt like a physical weight.

"We should move soon," Daniel said, checking his watch. "Still need to get through Portland before dark."

"South Portland," Hannah corrected quietly. "My family's in the Gardens. Near the airport."

Jessica began gathering their supplies with practiced efficiency. "We'll find them," she assured Hannah. "Then all head to the farm together."

Maddie helped clean up, noting how Daniel's attention had shifted to the northern horizon where the sun painted clouds in shades of orange and red. Or maybe that was smoke.

"Back in, everyone," he called. "Ryan, help your sister."

The truck's engine rumbled to life, the sound too loud in the evening quiet. As they merged back onto the empty interstate, Maddie caught Hannah's hand, squeezing gently. Whatever waited in South Portland, at least they weren't facing it alone anymore.

They drove steadily north as the sun sank lower, its light casting long shadows across the highway. The Portland Jetport's runway appeared to their left, eerily silent without its usual traffic. But as they turned onto Western Avenue, thick black smoke billowed ahead, marking trouble at the intersection.

"There." Hannah pointed, her voice tight. "James Baka Drive. We can cut through using the fire road."

Daniel slowed the truck, evaluating their options as flames licked the darkening sky. "You're sure about that access road?"

"Yes," Hannah's fingers dug into the seat. "Past the fire station. It'll take us right to the Gardens."

The smoke grew thicker as Daniel turned, everyone watching the flames paint the evening sky in shades of destruction.

The access road dead-ended at a heavy chain-link gate, a thick chain wrapped through its center.

"No," Hannah whispered, pressing against the window. "We're so close."

Daniel pulled the truck close to the gate, studying the barrier in the dying light. "Everyone stay inside." He grabbed the tire iron from behind the seat – the same one that had saved their lives in Portsmouth.

Metal screamed against metal as he worked the chain, each sound making them all flinch. Finally, the link snapped. Daniel dragged the gate open just wide enough for the truck, then carefully threaded the chain back through to appear intact from a distance.

"Smart," Jessica murmured as he climbed back in. "In case we need to come back through."

They rolled forward slowly, the truck's headlights off. Hannah's breath caught as they rounded the corner. "There! Number two!" She pointed to a small duplex, her excitement faltering as they pulled into the empty driveway. "Wait... Dad's car should be here. He always parks right there."

Daniel started to say something, but Hannah was already throwing open the door. "Hannah, wait—"

She sprinted toward the house, all caution forgotten.

Maddie scrambled after her, heart pounding. Through the growing shadows, she saw Hannah fumble with her key, hands shaking so badly she could barely work the lock.

The door swung open into darkness. Hannah disappeared inside before Maddie could catch her arm. "Mom? Dad?" Her voice cracked with desperation. "Jake?"

Maddie followed her inside, the last light of day revealing what they both feared. Furniture overturned. Drawers pulled out and emptied. Cabinet doors hanging open. The remnants of someone else's desperate search scattered across every surface.

Hannah stood frozen in the middle of the chaos, her medical bag slipping from nerveless fingers to land among the debris of her childhood home.

Daniel

Hannah's Home—South Portland, Maine

THE EVENING AIR HUNG HEAVY WHILE DANIEL scanned the quiet street, his back to the truck where Ryan and Lily huddled together in the back seat. Jessica stood beside him, both watching the dark doorway where Hannah and Maddie had disappeared minutes ago.

"It's too quiet," he muttered, unconsciously flexing his injured arm. The cut throbbed beneath Hannah's careful bandaging, a reminder of Portsmouth's chaos and the swift descent into anarchy.

Jessica moved closer, her voice barely above a whisper. "Should you check on them?"

Before he could answer, a drawer crashed somewhere inside the house, followed by Hannah's muffled voice calling for her parents. Daniel's hand tightened on the tire iron he hadn't put down.

"We can't stay here long," he said, eyes constantly moving between the houses, the intersections, the growing shadows. "That smoke we saw? Someone's still around to start those fires. We don't see them but there are people and some of them could be dangerous. Portland is so much more than Portsmouth and this is not a good place to be."

"But where do we go?" Jessica's normally steady voice wavered slightly. "It'll be dark in an hour, maybe less. And these girls…"

"I know." Daniel caught his wife's eye, seeing his own worry reflected there. They'd saved these young women from immediate danger, but now what? The road to Cornish meant navigating through Westbrook, Gorham and other towns that could be as bad as Portsmouth, or worse.

"Daddy?" Lily's small voice carried from the truck. "I need to go potty."

Jessica glanced at the house, then back at Daniel. "We need to make a decision. Try to push through to the farm tonight, or find somewhere to hole up until morning?"

A car door slammed somewhere in the distance, the sound unnaturally loud in the evening quiet. Daniel shifted his stance, positioning himself between the noise and his family.

"The girls know the area," he reasoned quietly. "But driving at night…" He thought of the highway they'd navigated in full daylight, the constant weaving between abandoned vehicles. In darkness, they'd be even more vulnerable.

"If we stay, we need a better position than this," Jessica said, her real estate agent's eye evaluating their surroundings. "Too exposed here. Too many ways in."

Daniel nodded, already cataloging threats: multiple access points, poor visibility, unknown neighbors. And now the growing dark would hide anyone watching them. But the alternative meant navigating through unknown threats at night, with exhausted children and traumatized young women…

"We've got maybe forty minutes of decent light left," he said finally. "Not enough time to make it to Cornish safely. But we need to—"

A metallic clatter from inside the house made them both jump. Hannah's voice carried through the open door. "Jake? Are you up there?"

"Daniel." Jessica gripped his arm. "We need to get them out. Now."

He started forward, but movement near the truck stopped him. Ryan had pressed his face against the window, eyes wide with fear. Lily curled against her brother, Mr. Trunks clutched tight. The grip on him was almost physical.

"I can't leave you and the children alone," he said, torn between protecting his children and retrieving the girls.

Glass shattered somewhere down the street. Jessica's fingers dug deeper into his arm. Another crash from inside the house, followed by Hannah's increasingly frantic calls.

"Please," Jessica whispered. "Just get them and—"

She froze mid-sentence. Daniel followed her gaze to the duplex's other unit. There, in an upstairs window, a face watched them through a gap in the curtains. The observer made no attempt to hide, just stared with an intensity that made Daniel's skin crawl.

"Get in the truck," he said quietly, never taking his eyes off the window.

"But the girls—"

"Now, Jess."

More sounds from inside Hannah's house seemed to echo through the empty space. Drawers opening, footsteps on stairs. Hannah's voice had taken on a desperate edge: "Dad? Mom? Someone answer me!"

The face in the window hadn't moved, hadn't blinked. Just

watched. Calculating. Waiting.

A door slammed somewhere behind them. Then another. The street had felt empty minutes ago, but now…

"Oh God," Jessica breathed. "Daniel, there's more of them."

He saw them now—shadows moving between houses, figures appearing in windows. They'd stayed too long. Let their guard down. And now they were being surrounded.

Hannah's voice cracked with panic. "Jake's computer is gone! Everything's gone!"

Daniel's mind raced. Go in after the girls and leave his family exposed? Stay with the truck and hope Maddie and Hannah emerged soon? Or the alternative, escape leaving them behind. The dying light painted everything in shades of threat, and that face kept watching, watching, watching…

The decision was immediate and without question. "Maddie! Hannah!" The shout burst from Daniel before he could stop himself. "We have to go!" His voice echoed between houses, drawing more shadows to windows, more faces emerging from darkened doorways.

Jessica backed toward the truck. "Daniel—"

"Get in. Lock the doors." He was already moving, the distance to Hannah's front door suddenly feeling endless. The tire iron felt slick in his sweating palm as he crossed the yard in long strides.

The face in the neighbor's window had disappeared.

He reached the doorway, heart thundering. Inside, he could hear the girls still moving through rooms, calling out. Too loud. Dammit, they were being too loud.

"We need to leave," he hissed into the darkness. "Right

now!"

"But Jake's room," Hannah's voice carried down the stairs.

"NOW!" The word came out sharper than he intended, edged with the panic he was trying to control.

Behind him, a door creaked. Then a voice called out, "Hey, what are you doing?"

Daniel spun, positioning himself in the doorway. A man stood on the neighbor's side of the porch; middle-aged, wearing what might have once been business casual but was now sweat-stained and dirty. He glanced around suddenly aware that others had emerged from surrounding houses, drawn by the commotion.

His mind raced through calculations and options. Jessica and the kids in the truck, the girls still inside, unknown threats closing in. The dying light and emerging aurora seemed to cast everything into shades of blood and shadow. They'd lingered too long, let themselves become surrounded, and now—

"I said, what are you doing?" The neighbor's voice carried a dangerous edge. More figures appeared behind him, moving with purpose.

Daniel raised his hands slowly, aware of the tire iron still gripped in one fist. "Listen, buddy. We're not trying to steal or anything. One of the girls we found—"

"You found girls?" The neighbor's face twisted with disgust. "What kind of person are you?" His voice trailed off as he craned to look at Jessica and the kids peering through the truck windows. Others muttered behind him, the sound ugly and threatening. "Driving around 'finding' girls? Looks like kids too?"

"No, wait—" Daniel felt the situation slipping away from

him. "You don't understand. We're just trying to—"

"Trying to what?" The first neighbor took another step forward. More figures emerged from surrounding houses, drawn by the confrontation.

"Oh hey, Mr. Ashford!" Hannah appeared in the doorway behind Daniel. "Have you seen my parents?"

The change in the atmosphere was instant. The neighbor—Mr. Ashford—sagged with visible relief. "Hannah? Hannah Mitchell? Thank God." He moved forward, but differently now; concern replacing suspicion. "We've been worried sick! Your parents—"

"Where are they?" Hannah cut in, hope and fear mixing in her voice. "They're not…" she paused, her hand going to her throat, "are they okay?"

Voices rose from the gathering crowd, overlapping in their rush to speak. "When did you get back?"

"We thought you were stuck in Boston!"

"Your mother was so worried—"

"Tom's been looking everywhere—"

Daniel felt the tension drain from his shoulders as the neighbors' focus shifted from threat to concern. Behind him, he heard Maddie join Hannah in the doorway, both girls suddenly surrounded by a community transforming from hostile to protective in the space of a heartbeat.

"HANNAH!"

The cry cut through the murmuring crowd. A woman burst between houses, running across the lawn with a speed that belied her age, her graying hair coming loose from its bun.

"MOM!" Hannah flew off the porch, nearly stumbling in her desperation to reach her mother. They collided in the yard, both dissolving into tears as they clutched each other. "Mom, oh God, Mom—"

"My baby," Mrs. Mitchell sobbed, rocking her daughter like she was still a child. "We tried to get to Boston—the cars wouldn't work. Oh lord, we thought. We thought…" She pulled back just enough to cover Hannah's face with kisses, then hugged her tight again.

Jessica's arm laced through his as she stepped up to join him, their own children peering from the truck's windows at the reunion. The neighbors' expressions had transformed completely, hostility replaced by relief and joy.

Mr. Ashford stepped forward, extending his hand to Daniel. "I'm so sorry about before. We've had… Well, we've seen some trouble. But bringing Hannah home…" He shook his head, emotion clouding his voice. "Thank you. Just… thank you."

Mrs. Mitchell finally loosened her grip on Hannah, though she kept one arm firmly around her daughter as she approached Daniel and Jessica. "You brought our girl home? Through everything that's happening?" Tears streamed down her face. "Please, you'll stay with us tonight. It's not safe to travel after dark, and we'll make room—Tom's got the generator running up the street, and there's food."

"Mom, where are dad and Jake? Our home?"

"It was broken into the day after everything happened. We went to look for a vehicle so that we could go find you. That didn't go well," she paused with a sigh, "When we got back we found it trashed. With the broken windows and door locks we moved over to the empty unit up on Wainwright. The whole building was empty. We can put your friends up in the other side."

Another neighbor spoke up, "We've been working to close off the entire community."

Daniel grimaced. "I may have messed up your security on the fire access road. We had to use it to get in and broke the chain."

"Good to know," the man said, "We knew it wouldn't last. We'd planned to put some vehicles across the road. Speaking of which, how do you have a running truck?"

"It is pre-computer chip. You should look for older vehicles," Daniel said, glancing skyward, thinking for a moment. "I'd say anything before 1980 might still work."

"Oh, excellent," he exclaimed, "I know of a couple we might be able to get going."

The offer of shelter, of safety, seemed to break something open in the gathering. Neighbors stepped forward with their own offerings. "I've got extra blankets—"

"Maize just made bread!"

"The kids must be hungry."

Daniel met Jessica's eyes, saw his own relief reflected there. They'd found more than shelter for the night. They'd found, however briefly, a pocket of humanity still intact.

Day Four—Cornish, Maine

THE FLOORBOARDS CREAKED BENEATH JAMES' FEET as he descended the stairs in the predawn darkness. Sarah's shadow moved through the kitchen below, outlined by the weak glow of a camping lantern. She hadn't slept again - he'd felt her tossing all night, muttering Daniel's name in her restless dreams.

"You're up early," he said softly, though they both knew she'd never gone to bed.

Sarah's hands never stopped moving as she worked biscuit dough on the counter. Her fingers pressed deep divots into the pale flour-dusted surface, each push and fold more aggressive than necessary. The kitchen already felt oppressive, July's humidity seeping through the window screens to coat everything in a fine sheen of moisture.

"Mrs. Miller mentioned wanting to check the garden today," Sarah said, her voice too bright, too controlled. "And Elena needs a proper breakfast. That poor girl can barely keep anything down." Her movements grew more forceful, the dough taking the brunt of her unspoken fears.

James stepped closer, noting the dark circles under his

wife's eyes, the slight tremor in her normally steady hands. "Sarah---"

"Don't." The word came sharp as a knife. "Just… don't. I need to get these in the oven before everyone wakes up." She turned away, shoulders rigid. "The gas stove's such a blessing. I don't know what we'd do without it. Though the propane won't last forever, will it? Another thing to worry about. Another thing to---" Her voice cracked.

The morning's first hints of light filtered through the windows as footsteps echoed from above - Emily already up, probably checking on Elena. The house would soon fill with their expanding group, each person carrying their own fears, their own needs. James watched Sarah straighten her spine, pulling her mask of efficiency back into place.

"I should check the freezer again," he said carefully. "Even in the basement, this heat…"

Sarah's hands stilled in the dough. "I keep thinking about all that meat. All those vegetables we put up last fall." She didn't turn around. "Daniel loved my strawberry preserves. Used to eat them right from the jar when he was little, remember? His chin all sticky and red…"

More footsteps overhead. The day was beginning whether they were ready or not. James touched Sarah's shoulder gently, feeling the tension thrumming through her body. "We'll figure it out. We always do."

The screen door's hinges protested as Michael entered, already sweating from his morning perimeter check. "No sign of trouble," he reported quietly. "But Frank Wilson's truck is parked down by the old Miller place. Been there since dawn."

James nodded, thoughts already racing. Frank's presence never meant anything good, but they had more immediate concerns. The freezer. The growing number of people depending on them. The suffocating heat that promised another scorcher of a day.

"Breakfast in thirty minutes," Sarah announced, her voice steady once more. "Michael, make sure Marianne has help getting down the stairs. And Emily will need more clean bandages for these damn cuts and blisters you all keep getting - check the linen closet, the old sheets can be torn up."

James took in the scene as his wife directed their expanding household with practiced efficiency, as if they were preparing for a holiday gathering rather than trying to survive the end of their world. He knew her well enough to see the cracks in her performance - the way her hands shook slightly as she worked, how her voice lifted too high when she spoke of Daniel.

But for now, there were biscuits to bake and a household to feed. The deeper worries would have to wait.

The kitchen filled gradually as morning crept forward. Emily helped Elena settle at the table, the pregnant woman's face pale in the strengthening light. Marianne Miller moved with careful dignity despite Michael's hovering assistance, her silver hair neatly pinned despite everything. The children's voices carried from upstairs where Matthew helped them dress.

"The garden needs attention," Marianne said, accepting a cup of coffee from Sarah. "And that freezer won't keep much longer, even in the basement. We'll need to act fast if we want to save anything."

Sarah's hands tightened on the coffee pot. "I was thinking, about it and you're right, but we are going to need canning supplies. With all those beautiful preserves you used to bring to the church suppers…I thought maybe you would know the best place."

"I have everything we need," Marianne chirped almost like the birds outside. "Jars, lids, the big pressure canner. George always teased me about keeping so much, but…" Her voice faltered slightly at her husband's name.

The screen door creaked again when a soft knock alerted them to a presence. Frank Wilson's bulk filled the doorway, his usual dishevelment somewhat muted. James noted how his hands stayed carefully visible, how his stance suggested submission rather than his usual swagger.

"Morning," Frank said with a tinge of contriteness. "Brought something that might help." He gestured toward his truck. "Got a smoker. One of them big commercial ones from the Elks Lodge. Figured with all this heat, might be useful for preserving meat."

The kitchen fell silent. James studied Frank carefully, seeing past the forced humility to something calculating in his bloodshot eyes. But they did need a smoker. And Frank's knowledge of preserving meat was well-known in the hunting community.

"That's mighty thoughtful," Marianne said into the silence. "Smoking and canning together, we might just save most of that freezer."

Steam curled from coffee cups as an uneasy silence settled over the kitchen. Frank remained in the doorway, his body language carefully submissive, though James caught the quick darting of his eyes - taking inventory, calculating resources.

"Might need help getting it set up," Frank offered, his voice lacking its usual belligerent edge. "But she's a good unit. Can handle a lot of meat at once."

Sarah's hands moved mechanically, setting out plates as Sophia and Ethan thundered down the stairs, their childhood energy a stark contrast to the adults' tension. The children stopped short at the sight of Frank, pressing closer to their mother.

"The freezer's got three deer, plus all last fall's pork," James said carefully. "Not to mention Sarah's garden vegetables." He watched Frank's reaction, noting how the man's fingers twitched at the mention of their food stores.

"That's a lot to process," Frank nodded, scratching his stubbled jaw. "Need plenty of hands. Plenty of fuel, too." He paused deliberately. "Got some oak wood seasoning behind the tavern. Perfect for smoking meat."

Michael shifted closer to Emily and the children, his need to protect evident in his positioning. "Awful convenient timing," he said, voice neutral but eyes sharp.

The July heat pressed harder against the windows as the sun climbed higher. Sweat beaded on Frank's forehead, though James suspected it wasn't entirely from the temperature.

"Look," Frank spread his hands. "I know what people think of me. Know I ain't been..." he glanced at the children, adjusting his language, "...the most upstanding citizen. But times like these, we all gotta pull together, right?"

"Of course we do," Marianne said firmly, her dignity somehow making the simple kitchen feel like a proper dining room. "James, the meat won't wait in this heat. And Sarah, dear, those biscuits smell ready."

Sarah started, turning to the oven she'd nearly forgotten. The scent of fresh biscuits filled the kitchen as she pulled them out, the familiar action steadying her slightly.

"We'll need more hands than just us," James said finally. "Smoking, canning - it's all got to happen fast." He met Frank's eyes. "You're right about working together."

"I could gather some folks," Frank offered quickly. "People I trust. Got a couple fellas who used to work the butcher counter at Shop & Save."

Elena made a small sound of distress at the mention of butchering. Matthew immediately moved to her side, but Emily was faster.

"Deep breaths," Emily soothed. "Focus on your breakfast. The baby needs strength."

James sipped his coffee silently, observing the interplay of relationships around his kitchen; his family's tight bonds, Marianne's quiet strength, Frank's calculated helpfulness. The room felt overwhelmed with competing needs and unstated fears.

"We'll need to coordinate with Beth," Michael said. "Extra people coming and going—we need proper security." His hand rested casually near his hip where James knew he carried his service weapon.

"Already spoke to her," Frank said, too quickly. "She's got her hands full down at the feed store. Trying to organize distribution, now the Portland gang's pulled back." He shifted his weight. "Figured this here's a way I can help. Put some of my…" he paused again, "…connections to good use."

Sarah placed a basket of biscuits on the table with more force than necessary. "Well, we're not doing anything without breakfast first. Frank, you might as well come in and eat. Wash up at the sink." Like an errant child she scolded him.

"Yes, Ma'am. Thank you Ma—"

"Oh knock off the ma'am garbage and have a seat over there, next to James."

Her voice carried that brittle brightness again. "Everyone sit. Grace before meals, same as always."

James was concerned with how Sarah struggled to maintain their normal routine like a shield against chaos. Keeping order through shared meals and proper manners, as if civilization might hold together through sheer force of will.

"Got some coffee, too," Frank added, gesturing toward his truck again. "Real coffee, not that instant stuff. Thought the ladies might appreciate it." His eyes flickered to Sarah, then away.

The morning light strengthened, highlighting the exhaustion on every face. James could almost see the calculations running behind Frank's bloodshot eyes—how much help to offer, how to make himself essential, how to secure his place in their emerging community.

"After breakfast," James decided, "Michael and I will check out this smoker. Sarah, you and Marianne can inventory what we need from her house for canning." He turned to Frank. "We'll need that wood you mentioned. And Frank? Those men you said could help? They need to understand—this is about community. About helping each other."

"Course," Frank nodded eagerly. "That's just what I was thinking. Community. Working together."

But something shifted behind his eyes, a calculation, a measurement of power and influence. James couldn't quite put his finger on it, but the calculation, timing and attitude made him question what Frank hoped to gain. Everyone knew Frank, and with him, everything came at a price. There was no denying they needed the help if they were going to save the freezer contents but how high the price might be was what worried James.

The kitchen filled with the sounds of breakfast—plates clinking, children whispering, Elena's soft murmur of thanks as Emily helped her with fresh tea. But beneath the domestic noise, James felt the currents of change. Frank Wilson, offering help with one hand while likely holding plans of his own in the other. Sarah, serving breakfast with mechanical precision while worry ate at her heart. And somewhere out there, Daniel's family, still making their way toward home.

The July sun climbed higher, promising another day of oppressive heat. They had meat to smoke, vegetables to can, and a community to hold together. James watched Frank settle at the edge of their table, accepted but not trusted, useful but not welcomed.

Sarah's hands shook slightly as she poured coffee into Frank's offered cup. "Eat up," Sarah said, her voice too bright. "We've got a long day ahead."

The clinking of forks against plates filled the brief silence as everyone ate. Even Frank seemed to sense the need for quiet, taking small bites of his biscuit between furtive glances around the table.

"That smoker," James said finally, setting down his coffee cup. "How long to get it set up?"

"Couple hours, maybe less with good help." Frank dabbed his mouth with a napkin - a strangely genteel gesture from a man usually seen wiping his face on his sleeve. "Got it hitched proper, just needs leveling and the chimney assembled."

Michael set his cup down deliberately. "I'll help James get it positioned, then we can take your truck for that oak wood." His tone made it clear this wasn't a suggestion but a strategy - keeping Frank in sight, under control.

"My canning supplies are all organized," Marianne offered.

"In the basement pantry, everything labeled. Matthew, dear, you and your mother could help me gather it all?"

Matthew glanced at Elena, his usual hovering instinct visible in his tense shoulders. Emily touched his arm gently. "Elena can help me here. Light duties only, I promise."

"The chickens need tending," Sarah added, her voice steadying as she focused on practical tasks. "Sophia, you and Ethan are the official chicken tenders and have been doing so well with them."

The children giggled at the chicken tender comment. "Can we name them?" Ethan asked around a mouthful of biscuit. "The black one looks like a Betty."

Matthew quipped, "Yea, one will be Nugget, another can be Stew, we can have a couple we call Pot and Pie."

A ghost of a real smile touched Sarah's lips, and she winked at Matthew. "We'll see. But first, they need fresh water and feed. You need to collect the eggs and the coop needs cleaning."

James watched his family separate into their tasks, standing back with a feeling of hope. Each person stepping up and finding purpose in the work ahead. But his mind kept straying to the road south, imagining Daniel's family fighting their way through who knew what dangers. Four days now. Four days of silence.

"I'll send some boys to patrol down toward Route 25," Frank offered, as if reading James' thoughts. "Keep an eye out for any visitors, friendly or otherwise."

The loaded word—visitors—hung in the air. James caught Sarah's slight flinch, saw how her hands tightened on the plate she was clearing.

"Let's focus on what's in front of us. We will leave security up to Beth and discuss it with her later," James said firmly, standing. "Michael, we'll get that smoker set up first. Matthew, give your mother and Mrs. Miller whatever help they need. Emily, don't let Elena do too much." He turned to Frank. "That wood needs to be good and dry. No green oak - it'll ruin the meat."

"Course," Frank nodded eagerly. "Got it seasoned proper. Dry as bone."

The breakfast dishes clattered as Sarah gathered them with mechanical precision, each movement carefully controlled. James wanted to comfort her, to promise Daniel would arrive any day now. But false hope could be more cruel than honest uncertainty.

Instead, he touched her shoulder gently as he passed. "We'll get through this," he said quietly. "One task at a time."

She nodded without looking up, her hands never stopping their endless work of maintaining order in their disordered world. Outside, the sun climbed higher, promising another brutally hot day. They had meat to save, supplies to gather, and a community to build…even if that meant cautiously accepting help from men like Frank Wilson.

But as James stepped onto the porch, following Frank and Michael toward the waiting smoker, his eyes strayed southward. Somewhere out there, his son was trying to reach them. All James could do was make sure there was still a home, still a community, for Daniel to find.

If he made it at all.

Maddie

Day Five—South Portland

HANNAH'S HANDS TREMBLED AS SHE FOLDED THE same t-shirt for the third time, her movements mechanical, uncertain. The pale morning light filtering through the nearly vacant bedroom window cast strange shadows across the small pile of clothes she'd assembled and disassembled countless times since dawn. A faded field hockey championship shirt - the one they'd both worn during their last summer camp together. Their matching Harvard University sweatshirts from the campus tour that felt like a lifetime ago.

"You don't have to decide right now," Maddie said softly, though they both knew that wasn't true. The sun climbing over South Portland subdivision's deceptively quiet streets marked their dwindling time.

Hannah's fingers traced the letters on the sweatshirt. "I can't just leave them." Her voice cracked. "Mom's finally stopped hanging on to me like I was a figment of her imagination and Dad's organizing the neighborhood watch. Jake…" She swallowed hard. "He needs his big sister."

Downstairs, the sound of Daniel checking the truck's engine carried through the open window. The steady mechanical rhythm punctuated by Jessica's voice organizing the children, keeping them busy to mask the tension of their imminent departure.

"I know." Maddie moved to the window, watching Ryan help his father while Lily clutched Mr. Trunks, her small face solemn in the morning light. "But after what we saw in Portsmouth…" The words caught in her throat, Grace's final scream still echoed in her nightmares.

Hannah abandoned the t-shirt, crossing to grip Maddie's arms. "Listen to me. We're going to convince them. Maybe not today, but soon. Dad's smart - he'll see what's coming." Her fingers dug in almost painfully. "This isn't goodbye. It's just… see you later."

The sound of boots on the stairs made them both turn. Daniel appeared in the doorway, his injured arm held carefully against his side. "We need to move soon. Those fires we saw last night are spreading west."

Hannah's mother appeared behind him, her face lined with worry she'd been working so hard to hide. "At least stay for breakfast. I made pancakes - real ones, with the last of our maple syrup." Her forced cheer couldn't quite mask the tremor in her voice.

This ripped at Maddie's heart. 'The last of our Maple Syrup' spoke volumes about their position here. They didn't even have enough food, but were willing to give away what they had.

"Mom…" Hannah's composure cracked. She flew into her mother's arms, both women clutching each other as if they could freeze time through sheer force of will.

"I'll be downstairs, Maddie. See you in a few minutes," Daniel said, turning to go back down.

Maddie turned to the window, her own eyes burning. Through the glass, she fixated on Jessica comforting Lily, smoothing the little girl's hair. The simple gesture made her throat tighten as she thought of her own mother, wondering if she was doing the same things back in Cornish. Trying to maintain normalcy in a world that had shattered around them.

The smell of pancakes and woodsmoke drifted up from downstairs, mixing with the acrid scent of distant fires. Hannah's father's voice carried from the kitchen, deep in discussion with Daniel about routes and alternatives. The mundane morning sounds felt like a mockery of their last moments together.

"We should head down," Hannah said finally, wiping her eyes. "Help Mom with breakfast."

But neither of them moved. Instead, they stood frozen in the vacant room. Small bed pallets lined one each side of the wall and a pile of Hannah's clothes sat on the floor.

The world was ending, had already ended, and all they could do was fold and refold the same t-shirt, pretending they had any real choice in what came next.

Hannah's fingers traced the unfamiliar windowsill, her movements hesitant in this borrowed space.

"Does it feel weird?" Maddie asked, watching her friend navigate the foreign terrain of this temporary shelter. "Being here instead of your house?"

"Everything feels weird." Hannah's laugh held no humor. She gestured at the generic beige walls, the strange floral curtains left by previous tenants. "Mom tried to make it feel like home, but…" She trailed off, her eyes fixed on the window where thin streams of smoke rose in the distance.

Daniel's voice carried up the narrow stairwell. "Twenty minutes. We need to be on the road before that smoke gets any closer."

The kitchen below felt crowded with too many people trying to maintain normal routines in abnormal circumstances. Hannah's mother worked the camping stove they'd set up on the counter, the blue flame casting dancing shadows as she flipped pancakes. Her movements were too careful, too measured, like an actress performing domesticity on an unfamiliar stage.

"Eat while they're hot," she urged, stacking plates high. Her forced cheer couldn't quite mask how her hands shook. "Growing girls need a proper breakfast."

Hannah's father stood by the window, his rifle propped in the corner as he studied the street below. Two young men from their makeshift community patrolled the perimeter, their own weapons clearly visible. The single mother from three doors down hurried past with her children, heading for the common kitchen they'd established in an adjacent home.

"The route through Westbrook looks clearest," Daniel said, spreading his map across the unfamiliar kitchen table. "If we stick to back roads—"

"You could stay," Hannah's mother interrupted, her spatula hovering mid-flip. "We're organizing here. Setting up security. Tessa is teaching the children in the basement, trying to keep things normal. We have some food, supplies…"

"For now." Daniel's voice was gentle but firm. "But we saw what's coming. Portsmouth was just the beginning."

"Mom," Hannah started, but her voice cracked. She gripped Maddie's hand under the table, fingers intertwining with desperate strength.

The sound of breaking glass echoed from somewhere in the distance, followed by shouts. Hannah's father moved to the window, rifle ready, but the noise faded.

"Getting closer," he muttered, exchanging a look with Daniel that carried volumes of unspoken concern.

Jessica gathered Lily closer, helping her cut the pancakes into careful squares. Ryan sat rigid beside his sister, his young face too serious as he watched the adults' silent communications. The boy had aged years in only days, Maddie realized. They all had.

They wasted no time in eating and quickly prepared to leave. Outside, Daniel's truck idled in the early morning heat, the engine's rumble drawing worried glances from others in their makeshift community. A small crowd had gathered. The single mother clutching her children close, the younger woman Hannah clearly distrusted and had confided in Maddie yesterday, was what she called a user—hanging back with calculating eyes. There was the older couple who'd helped organize their night patrols.

"Last chance," Daniel said quietly, checking his watch and winding it quietly in a moment of forced habit. The smoke on the horizon had thickened, curling like dark fingers reaching toward them. "Anyone who wants to come…"

Hannah's father cleared his throat. "We've built something here. A community. People need us." But his eyes strayed to the smoke, uncertainty crossing his weathered face.

"Then take this." Daniel pressed a folded paper into his hand. "If things get worse—when things get worse—come to Cornish. To the Thompson farm. Show them this note, tell them Daniel sent you." His voice dropped lower. "Don't trust the main roads."

"You have to convince them," Maddie whispered as she embraced Hannah. "Promise me you'll try."

"I promise." Hannah's voice broke. "Promise to be safe?"

"I will." The lies caught in Maddie's throat, they both knew safety no longer existed. Instead, she hugged her friend harder, trying to memorize the feeling of having someone who knew all her stories, who remembered who she used to be.

"We need to move," Daniel called softly. "Daylight's burning."

Jessica helped the children into the truck, Lily still clutching Mr. Trunks with white-knuckled fingers. Ryan pressed his face against the window, waving sadly at the friends he'd made in their brief stay.

The goodbye stretched like pulled taffy - too long and not long enough. Finally, Hannah stepped back, her mother's arm around her shoulders. They looked small suddenly, standing in front of the borrowed apartment building that wasn't really home.

As Maddie climbed into the truck, she heard Hannah's voice one last time: "Remember the handkerchief! Martha said it was for luck!"

The words hit her like a physical blow—Martha's handkerchief, still tucked in her pocket. Martha, who had saved them, and stayed behind in Boston. Like Hannah was staying behind now. Like Grace had stayed behind forever in that dark harbor water.

The truck pulled away, and Maddie watched out the window as Hannah's figure grew smaller, one hand raised in farewell. She kept watching until they turned the corner, until the last glimpse of her friend disappeared like smoke into the morning air.

The truck wound through South Portland's back streets, each turn taking them further from Hannah and closer to whatever waited ahead. The morning heat pressed against the windows, making the cab feel smaller, more confined. Lily had finally stopped crying, though she still huddled against her brother, Mr. Trunks squeezed between them.

"You okay?" Jessica asked softly, reaching back to touch Maddie's knee.

Maddie nodded, not trusting her voice. The handkerchief in her pocket felt impossibly heavy, weighted with too many goodbyes.

"We'll take Highland Avenue," Daniel said, his attention fixed on navigating around abandoned vehicles. "Avoid the main routes into Westbrook. Less likely to run into-" He cut himself off, glancing at the children.

The silence stretched as they passed through neighborhoods showing increasing signs of violence - broken windows, doors hanging open, occasional dark stains on pavement that Maddie tried not to examine too closely. The smoke from distant fires cast everything in a hazy unreality.

"Look!" Ryan pointed suddenly. "Horses!"

Two well-groomed horses stood in a front yard, still wearing their riding tack. No riders in sight. The animals lifted their heads as the truck passed, ears pricked forward with interest.

"Dad?" Lily's voice wavered. "Can we have a horse at Grandpa's farm?"

"We'll see, Princess." Daniel navigated carefully through Westbrook's side streets. Evidence of looting marked some buildings, but the worst damage seemed concentrated around the larger stores. They wound through residential areas, keeping to the quieter roads.

"Almost through," Daniel said, tension easing slightly as they cleared the town limits. "That wasn't as bad as I expected."

Jessica relaxed her grip on the door handle. "Maybe people are staying home, trying to wait it out."

They made good time on the back roads toward Standish, the morning sun climbing higher as fields and scattered houses replaced urban sprawl. Maddie felt herself starting to hope - another hour, maybe less, and they'd reach Cornish.

The illusion of safety shattered as they rounded a curve near Standish center. Movement in the trees caught Maddie's eye - figures moving with purpose, weapons visible.

"Isn't that Mr. Masters?" she asked, squinting at a familiar silhouette.

"Sherman?" Daniel cursed, recognition flooding his face. "What's he doing with this bunch?" He eased off the gas, trying not to draw attention as he scanned for an escape route.

Too late. A shout went up from the trees, followed by the crack of gunfire. Daniel yanked the wheel hard, cutting down a narrow logging road as bullets sparked off the truck's frame.

The engine took a hit somewhere in that first barrage, steam erupting from under the hood as Daniel fought to keep control. They made it maybe half a mile before the truck shuddered to a final stop.

"Out!" Daniel grabbed his bug-out bag from behind the seat. "Into the woods! Now!"

They ran, bullets cutting through branches around them. Lily stumbled, Mr. Trunks falling from her grasp. Ryan snatched the elephant up without breaking stride, shoving it into his sister's arms as they crashed through underbrush.

Behind them, voices carried clearly: "Check the truck! Get those supplies!"

They pressed deeper into the woods, moving as quietly as possible while putting distance between themselves and the road. Finally, Daniel called a halt in a small hollow screened by thick pines.

Lily's muffled sobs mixed with the distant sound of men ransacking their truck. All their supplies, their food, their water—everything but Daniel's bug-out bag and Hannah's small medical kit; now in the hands of Sherman's gang.

"What do we do now?" Ryan whispered, holding his sister close.

Daniel met Jessica's eyes over their children's heads, then glanced at Maddie. They all knew - on foot, minimal supplies, at least ten miles from Cornish through territory clearly controlled by hostile people.

Lily pressed her face into Mr. Trunks' worn fur, trying to muffle her crying as voices carried through the trees: "Spread out! Find their trail!"

Maddie clutched Martha's handkerchief in her pocket, thinking of Hannah's last words about luck. They were going to need more than luck now. They were going to need a miracle.

Daniel

Day 5—Almost Home

DANIEL PRESSED ANOTHER LEAFY MAPLE BRANCH against the fallen oak's trunk, carefully obscuring the hollow beneath where Jessica lay, her newly broken ankle supported by their makeshift splint. The injury was less than an hour old, but every tiny movement had drawn sharp gasps of pain from her usually stoic demeanor. Lily curled against her mother's side, Mr. Trunks clutched tight, while Ryan sat watch with solemn eyes. Maddie crouched at the entrance, Hannah's medical kit open beside her as she adjusted the wrapping.

"I won't be long," he whispered, shrugging off the fully-stocked bug-out bag. "Everything you might need is in here. Water, protein bars, first aid supplies." His throat burned with thirst, but he pushed away the water bottle Jessica tried to hand him. "Save it. The kids need it more."

"Daniel." Jessica's voice was tight with pain. "Please be careful."

He touched her cheek, forcing himself to appear calmer than he felt. Dappled sunlight through sugar maples and birch painted shifting patterns across her face. "Rest. Try not to move that ankle." His eyes met Maddie's. "Any movement, any sound—"

"We'll stay quiet," she promised. "We know."

Ryan's small hand gripped his arm. "Dad?"

Daniel pulled his son close, remembering countless games of hide and seek in their Lynnfield backyard. But this was no game. "Watch out for your mom and sister, Buddy. You're in charge while I'm gone."

Moving through the dense New England forest required more attention than he'd expected.

Daniel broke another small branch at shoulder height, careful to make it look natural while still marking his path back to Jessica and the kids. His mind worked through their position—they'd abandoned the truck near the Standish roundabout at Higgins Corner, then moved almost due west through the woods. The Saco River was their biggest obstacle, and it was a big one. They'd need Route 25 to cross it, unless they wanted to risk swimming—impossible with Jessica's broken ankle. A rather quick river, deep and wide, difficult to ford even by the strongest. The kids could never make it. All he could hope was the bridge was open.

The woods couldn't be more than a few miles wide in any direction, but that was almost worse. Too easy to stumble into someone's backyard, or cross one of the scattered roads that cut through the forest. Every rustle of leaves made him pause, aware that civilization pressed close despite the illusion of wilderness.

A wide patch of blueberries scratched against his legs, and he wished they were ripe as he worked through another dense patch of underbrush. The mix of maples, birch, and pine provided decent cover, but also limited visibility. He froze at the sound of a car door slamming somewhere ahead—the first working vehicle he'd heard since Sherman's men had disabled their truck.

A glint of sunlight on metal caught his eye. He dropped instinctively, pressing against cool earth as voices carried through the trees. It was the road. Had to be Route 25. He crawled forward on his elbows, the childhood games of soldier he'd played feeling like poor preparation for this moment.

A massive granite boulder provided cover at the forest's edge. Daniel pressed against it, controlling his breathing as heavy boots crunched on asphalt. The voices grew clearer.

"—whole world's dark now. That guy on the radio ain't lying. No power anywhere."

"Makes it easier for us. While everyone's waiting for the lights to come back on, we take what we want."

Laughter. The sound made Daniel's skin crawl. "Gonna get me a couple of women. That pretty thing over in Standish been catching my eye. You know, the one from the coffee shop?"

"Save some for the rest of us. Once we clear out Cornish—"

"That farm up on Pound Hill first. Heard they got some woman treating people. Probably got medicines stored up."

Daniel's fingers dug into soft earth as he fought the urge to reveal himself. Could the woman they mentioned be his sister Emily? Had she found her way to their father's farm? Four men, heavily armed, strolled down the road like they owned it. Rifles slung casual but ready. Handguns visible on belts.

"Gonna be kings," one said, his boots scuffing asphalt. "Ain't nobody can stop us now. Government's gone. Police gone. Just us and what we can take."

Their voices faded as they moved south, but their words burned in Daniel's mind. Someone treating people at his father's farm. Stored supplies. Everything they might have built, everything they might have saved, now a target for men who saw the world's darkness as an opportunity.

He stayed frozen behind the boulder, mind racing. His family hidden and hurt less than a mile away. These men between them and safety. And somewhere ahead, his father's farm preparing for an attack they didn't know was coming.

The morning sun climbed higher, but Daniel felt cold despite the heat. They had to move soon. Had to get Jessica help. Had to warn whoever was at the farm. But one wrong step, one cry from Lily, one moment of bad luck, and they'd draw the attention of men who saw the apocalypse as their chance to become kings.

He checked his watch again. 10:45 AM. The minutes ticked by without his permission, filled with impossible choices and dwindling time.

Daniel kneeled by the boulder, scanning the highway again when Maddie touched his arm. She gestured him a few steps away, far enough that Jessica couldn't hear but still within sight.

"This isn't going to work," she whispered, her voice tight with concern. "You're already exhausted. I've watched you stagger twice in the last hundred yards."

"I can manage." The words came out harsher than he intended.

"When's the last time you drank anything? Or ate?" When he didn't answer, she pressed on. "Those pancakes were hours ago, and you gave your protein bar to Lily. In this heat, carrying Jessica…" She shook her head. "We need to find another way."

Daniel started to argue, but his trembling muscles betrayed him. "What do you suggest?"

"Look at all these abandoned vehicles. There has to be something—a bike, a cart, anything with wheels." She gestured toward River Road, visible through the trees. "We're almost to the Saco. The bridge can't be more than half a mile from here."

He scrubbed a hand across his face, wiping away sweat. "Keep watch? I'll scout ahead, see what I can find."

"Drink first." She thrust the water bottle at him. "You're no good to any of us if you collapse."

The water was warm but felt like heaven on his parched throat. He forced himself to take only small sips, knowing they needed to ration what remained.

Moving cautiously from vehicle to vehicle, Daniel worked his way along the roadside. Most had been picked clean, but across the street, something caught his eye. Behind a scorched SUV, half-hidden by burned debris, sat an old wheelbarrow. One wooden handle was broken, and the rubber tire was nearly flat, but…

He dragged it back across the road, staying low. The broken handle would make steering difficult, but Maddie's eyes lit up when she saw it.

"Perfect. We can use branches to make a seat, maybe extend it for her leg." She was already digging in the bug-out bag, pulling out paracord. "Ryan, help me find some straight branches about this long."

They worked quickly, lashing smaller branches together to create a makeshift seat. Another sturdy branch tied to the broken handle gave them better control. The half-flat tire would make the ride rough, but it beat carrying Jessica.

"It's not exactly a luxury sedan," Daniel said as they helped Jessica settle into their creation.

She managed a small smile despite her pain. "Better than being carried like a sack of potatoes."

The wheelbarrow creaked but held as Daniel lifted the handles. With Maddie steadying the broken side and the kids walking close beside them, they began their slow journey toward the bridge. It wasn't perfect, but it gave them a chance.

Behind them, the granite boulder stood silent sentinel over their abandoned hiding place, while ahead, the Saco River waited—their last major obstacle before reaching the farm. If they could make it across without being seen.

Daniel estimated at least eight hours ahead of them as they cleared the Saco River bridge, the wheelbarrow creaking with every bump. Under normal conditions, he could walk to his father's farm in four, but with Jessica's injury, the children's shorter strides, and the need to stay alert for threats, their progress would be painfully slow.

The afternoon heat pressed down as they moved through Limington. Most houses showed signs of life—curtains twitching, doors quickly closing, the occasional whispered conversation cutting off as they passed. Fear had turned neighbors into strangers, everyone retreating behind locked doors to protect what little they had left.

"Stop right there!" A man's voice rang out from a screened porch, followed by the unmistakable sound of a shotgun being racked.

Daniel froze, angling his body to shield Jessica in the wheelbarrow. Maddie pulled the children closer, her hands tight on their shoulders. The late afternoon sun cast long shadows across the yard as the screen door creaked open.

A man in his fifties emerged, shotgun trained steady. His eyes swept over their strange procession, lingering on Jessica's injured ankle, before settling on the children. Something in his expression shifted at the sight of Lily clutching Mr. Trunks, Ryan standing brave but trembling beside her.

"Shit," the man muttered, lowering his weapon slightly. "You got kids with you? Where you headed?"

"Cornish," Daniel said carefully. "My father's farm."

"Cornish?" The man frowned. "Don't know much about farms up that way."

The man disappeared inside briefly, returning with four plastic bottles of water. "Here," he said, tossing them over. "Ain't much, but you look like you could use it." His eyes swept the road in both directions. "Better hurry. Roads ain't safe after dark."

"Thank you," Jessica said softly from the wheelbarrow.

The man nodded once, then added quietly, "Good luck. All of you." Something in his tone suggested he understood more than he was saying about the state of things.

Daniel studied the man's face, making a quick decision. "I'm Daniel Thompson. My father's place is about 180 acres, outside town." He paused, then added, "Been hearing some troubling things. Armed men on the roads, talking about raids."

The man's grip tightened on his shotgun. "Heard some of that myself."

"Listen," Daniel said, his voice dropping, "if things get bad around here... if you need help..." He shifted his weight, conscious of Jessica's pain and the children's exhaustion. "Ask for Daniel in town."

The man dipped his head and disappeared back into his house but his eyes watched them through drawn curtains.

They continued on, the fresh water a blessing in the

oppressive heat. Behind them, the man stood watching until they rounded a bend, his shotgun still ready but no longer aimed at them. Daniel had seen the fear in his eyes—the same fear he'd seen in every face since the lights went out. But he'd also seen something else: recognition that they couldn't survive this new world alone.

The wheelbarrow creaked steadily onward as afternoon surrendered to evening.

Beth

Cornish—Day 5

BETH SAVORED THE LAST BITE OF HER CORNBREAD, made from Kristie's dwindling supply of ingredients. The small diner felt almost normal in the late afternoon heat—if you ignored the open windows replacing electric fans, and the limited menu scrawled on a piece of cardboard. The familiar smell of coffee and baked bread drifted from the massive oil stove that had been the diner's heart since the 1930s.

"Can't serve much," Kristie said, wiping down the counter with practiced movements. "But seems important to stay open. Give folks a place to remember how things were." She gestured toward the old stove, its blue-black surface radiating steady heat. "Grandfather insisted we keep it even after we got electric. Said you never know when you might need the old ways. Guess he was right."

Robbie Burns nodded from his seat beside Beth, his work-weathered hands wrapped around a coffee cup. "Some folks get it," he said, stirring honey into his coffee—real honey from the Wilsons' place, traded for meals. "Like Kristie here. Adapting but keeping what matters. Others…" He shook his head. "Still waiting for the power company to show up and fix everything."

"Then there's the ones who see opportunity," Beth added

quietly, thinking of Frank Wilson's growing influence. "The ones who knew exactly what they'd do when civilization's walls came down."

Kristie's hands stilled on the counter. "Had three different men offer to 'protect' my place this week. Wasn't protection they were offering."

"Want me to have a word?" Robbie straightened, his protective nature showing through. He'd been trying to help Beth maintain order since Jerry's injury, though he had no official standing.

"Handled it myself." Kristie's smile held steel beneath its warmth. "Amazing what a cast iron skillet and a clear aim can communicate. But they'll be back. Different ones, probably, but same intentions."

Beth pushed her empty plate away, mentally adding Kristie's situation to her growing list of concerns. "Think I'll take a ride out toward the preserve. Been meaning to check some possible barrier points, now that Jerry's laid up."

"I'll come with you," Robbie said immediately. "No sense patrolling alone these days."

She started to protest but stopped herself. Jerry's injury had shaken everyone, a stark reminder that her badge carried less authority each day. And Robbie was steady, reliable—even if his interest in her sometimes made things awkward.

"Coffee for the road?" Kristie offered, already reaching for thermoses. "Made fresh this morning on the old girl." She patted the oil stove affectionately.

"You should save it," Beth protested. "Coffee's getting scarce."

"That's exactly why I serve it." Kristie filled two thermoses with practiced efficiency. "Reminds people we're still civilized. Still neighbors." She wrapped the last of the cornbread in a cloth napkin, adding it to their thermoses. "Just… be careful out there. Things feel different today. Edgy."

Beth nodded, understanding the warning beneath Kristie's casual tone. The diner served as more than a place to eat—it was their community's pulse point, where whispered concerns and observed patterns painted a picture of growing threats.

"Ready?" Robbie stood, checking that his personal sidearm was secure from habit.

Beth gathered the thermoses, their warmth comforting against her palms. The late afternoon sun cast long shadows through the diner's windows as they stepped outside. The air felt heavy with more than just July heat.

Something was coming. She could feel it in the way people hurried through their tasks, in the nervous glances toward the road south. The preserve could wait. First, she needed to drive the perimeter, check their makeshift barriers, watch for whatever the day's lengthening shadows might be hiding.

Beside her, Robbie opened the cruiser's door, the hinges creaking in familiar protest. One of the last running vehicles in town, it served as both transportation and symbol—a reminder of order they fought daily to maintain.

The coffee's rich aroma filled the car as Beth started the engine. Its rumble drew the usual attention, curtains twitching in nearby houses. Everyone watching, always watching now.

The cruiser wound along Route 25, tires crunching over scattered debris. Beth pulled onto the shoulder near Charlie Wheeler's place, where the road narrowed between two steep banks.

"Natural bottleneck," Robbie observed, squinting in the late afternoon light. "Add some barriers here, funnel people where we can see them coming."

Charlie emerged from his barn, wiping grease from his hands. "Been thinking the same thing," he said, leaning against Beth's open window. "Got some concrete barriers from that construction site down in Standish. Could drag 'em up here, make a proper checkpoint."

Beth nodded, studying the terrain. "We'd need volunteers to—" She stopped, straightening suddenly. "You see that?"

Silhouettes appeared over the rise, dark shapes against the lowering sun. A group moving slowly down the middle of the road, something awkward being pushed between them.

"Stay here," she told Charlie. "We'll check it out."

The cruiser's engine rumbled to life. Beth flipped on the lights, muscle memory from hundreds of traffic stops. As they approached, she tapped the siren—a quick *bwip* that echoed off the trees.

The group froze. Details emerged through the heat shimmer: a makeshift wheelbarrow with one broken handle, a woman propped in it, two children pressed close to a young woman's sides. A man stood protective stance in front, his clothes dark with sweat.

"Daniel Thompson?" Beth stepped out of the cruiser slowly, taking in their bedraggled group with growing concern. "What in the world…"

"Chief Martin," Daniel's relief was palpable. "Jessica's hurt her ankle, we've been trying to—"

"Let's get you all in the car." Beth's voice was gentle but firm. "Your mother will be glad to see you."

"Everyone ok?" Daniel asked as Robbie helped ease Jessica from the wheelbarrow. "We were worried—"

"Everyone is fine. We'll have you there in no time." She turned to the young woman helping the children. "I don't believe we've met?"

"Maddie Foster," she said, steadying Lily as the little girl swayed with exhaustion. "My parents—the hardware store in town? I need to get home to them…"

Beth frowned slightly, the name tugging at her memory but not quite connecting. "Foster's Hardware… Yes, I know the place. Let's get everyone up to the Thompson place first. It's closer, and we can get Jessica some help. Then I promise we'll sort out getting you home."

"I can stay behind," Robbie offered, looking at the crowded car. "Give you more room."

"We'll manage," Beth said. "Everyone's tired enough without leaving anyone behind. Kids can sit on laps, we'll make it work."

They arranged themselves carefully—Jessica in front with Lily dozing in her lap, her ankle propped awkwardly. Daniel took the middle of the back seat with Ryan, while Maddie and Robbie squeezed in on either side.

"Old Limington Road's quickest," Beth said, starting the engine. "It'll be an easier road with all the other things going on. I've been meaning to have a look at it anyway."

The cruiser moved steadily through the late afternoon light, Beth keeping a moderate pace. No need to draw attention, but no need to dawdle either. The sun hung low, painting the western sky in shades of orange and pink.

"Not much further. Your family's sure gonna be glad to see

you." Beth smiled at them. "We'll get ya there."

"Thank you," Jessica said softly. "We weren't sure how much further we could go."

"All of you." She glanced in the rearview mirror at Maddie. "And we'll figure out about getting you to your folks right after we get them up to the Thompson place. We'll go find your parents. I just can't quite place which Fosters..."

"My dad's David Foster? Mom's Katherine?"

"Give me a bit - it'll come to me," Beth said warmly. "Town's been a bit chaotic lately. But we'll sort it out once we get Jessica settled."

The cruiser wound along Old Limington Road, its engine providing a steady background hum. Lily had fallen asleep clutching Mr. Trunks, while Ryan fought to keep his eyes open. The day's heat was finally beginning to fade, bringing the promise of evening's cooler air.

"Sorry about the bumps," Beth said as the cruiser turned onto the dirt road, her speed dropping to accommodate the uneven surface. Jessica winced as they hit another rut, trying to brace her ankle.

"Still better than the wheelbarrow," she managed with a weak smile.

Daniel leaned forward between the seats, pointing toward a natural narrowing where steep banks pressed close to the road. "That would make a good checkpoint," he said quietly. "Like a funnel."

Beth nodded. "Been thinking the same thing. Charlie Wheeler's got some concrete barriers. We could set up something proper." She navigated around a washout, the cruiser's tires crunching on loose gravel.

Lily stirred in Jessica's lap but didn't wake, Mr. Trunks still clutched tight. Ryan had finally lost his battle with exhaustion, slumped against Daniel's side. Only Maddie remained alert, her eyes constantly scanning the tree line as if expecting Grace to somehow appear.

"Your father's been worried," Beth said to Daniel, keeping her voice low to avoid waking the children. "Sarah, too, though she won't admit it. Just keeps cooking enough for an army."

Jessica's hand found Daniel's, squeezing tight. The simple gesture carried volumes—relief, exhaustion, hope.

The road wound higher, each familiar curve bringing them closer to home. Robbie pointed out fresh tire tracks crossing the dirt. "Getting more traffic up here lately," he observed. "People coming to Emily for medical help."

"Emily's at the farm?" Daniel's voice lifted with surprise.

Beth smiled. "A lot's happened while you were gone. Your sister's become quite the community doctor." She left out the darker parts—Jerry's injury, and early looting. The threats they feared might return. There'd be time for that later.

The late afternoon sun slanted through the trees as they crested the final hill. Beth could Daniel's shoulders relax in the rearview mirror at the sight of the familiar buildings, the barn's weathered red paint glowing in the golden light and for the first time in days she smiled. A genuine feeling of hope welling up inside her nearly bringing her to tears.

James emerged onto the porch, lifting a hand in greeting as the cruiser pulled into the yard. Dust rising as the tires kicked up the gravel before stopping. Beth couldn't help smiling as she stepped out, enjoying the moment.

"Got a present for you," she called up to the porch with a

wide grin on her face she couldn't conceal.

James

Thompson Farm

THE SCREEN DOOR'S HINGES PROTESTED AS JAMES stepped onto the porch, drawn by Beth's cruiser rumbling up the drive. Dust billowed golden in the late afternoon sun, obscuring the passengers, but something in Beth's posture as she emerged made his heart skip.

Then he saw him. Daniel, unfolding himself from the back seat, thinner than James remembered, clothes dark with sweat. For a moment, James couldn't breathe, couldn't move, couldn't process the miracle standing in his driveway.

"Sarah!" His voice cracked as he called back into the house. "Sarah, come out here! Everyone, come quick!"

He took the porch steps two at a time, bare feet slapping against sun-warmed wood. Daniel met him halfway, and James caught his son in a fierce embrace that nearly knocked them both off balance. Daniel smelled of sweat and pine needles and something metallic - like fear finally releasing its grip.

"Your mother's been baking for an army," James managed, his voice rough. Behind him, the screen door slammed.

Sarah's gasp cut through the evening air. "Daniel?" Her voice trembled, disbelief warring with desperate hope. "Oh God, Daniel!"

She flew past James, nearly bowling them both over as she threw her arms around their son. Her fingers clutched Daniel's shirt like she feared he might disappear if she let go. "My baby, my baby," she kept whispering, tears streaming unchecked down her face.

"Mom," Daniel's voice caught. "Dad. I'm sorry it took so long, but Jessica's hurt and—"

The mention of his wife seemed to break whatever spell had frozen the others by the car. Jessica looked up from where Robbie helped ease her from the front seat, her face tight with pain. Two small figures tumbled out after her - Lily clutching a well-loved stuffed elephant, Ryan hovering protective beside his sister.

"Emily!" James called toward the barn. "We need you out here!"

Sarah released Daniel just enough to spot her grandchildren. "Oh, look at you both," she breathed, opening her arms wider. Lily hesitated only a moment before running to her grandmother, Mr. Trunks bouncing against her leg. Ryan followed more slowly, his young face carrying shadows no child should know.

Emily burst from the barn, medical bag already in hand, Michael close behind her, both freezing at the sight of Daniel. Then Emily was running, nearly tripping over her own feet as she rushed to join the family cluster.

James stepped back, giving them space as emotions crashed over each other like waves. His eyes found Maddie standing alone by the cruiser, arms wrapped tight around herself, watching this family reunion with a mixture of hope and heartbreak that made his chest ache.

Marianne Miller emerged onto the porch, her silver hair

catching the evening light. Without hesitation, she moved to Maddie's side, placing a gentle hand on the girl's shoulder. "You helped bring them home," she said softly. "That makes you family, too."

"All of us," James called out, his voice carrying across the yard. "We weather this storm together." He gestured for Maddie to join them, watching relief flood her face as she stepped forward.

"Jessica needs attention first," Emily said, already kneeling to examine the swollen ankle. Her professional demeanor couldn't quite mask the tears in her eyes. "Let's get her inside where I can see this properly."

"Here, I've got her." Michael stepped forward, but Daniel shook his head.

"I'll carry my wife," he said firmly, though exhaustion lined every movement as he lifted Jessica. She wrapped her arms around his neck, pressing her face against his shoulder.

"The rest of you, too," Sarah commanded, one arm still around Ryan while Lily clung to her other hand. "Everyone inside. You all look half-starved." Her voice caught. "I've got biscuits warming and beef stew that's been simmering all day."

"We've set up a proper clinic in the barn," James said. "Better light, more space."

Emily nodded to them, already supporting Jessica's other side as Daniel helped her toward the converted storage room. The building's heavy doors creaked open, revealing neat shelves of medical supplies and a proper examination table - evidence of how much had changed in their short absence.

"Mom!" Sophia and Ethan burst from the house, stopping short at the sight of their unfamiliar cousins. Ryan and Lily pressed closer to Sarah, exhaustion and uncertainty written across their small faces.

"Hey," Sophia said, taking charge with all her ten-year-old confidence. "Want to see our chickens? We've got a black one named Betty who lets you pet her."

Lily's eyes widened, her grip on Mr. Trunks loosening slightly. "Real chickens?"

"Come on!" Ethan grabbed Ryan's hand. "We saved some eggs for collecting. You can help!"

Sarah called out to the children as they moved toward the coop, "Children, let's eat first."

They paused and Sophia called back. "Only be two minutes, Gram. Please?"

Something tight in her chest eased at the sound of Lily's first real giggle. "Alright. Two minutes," she warned. "The rest of you, inside," she commanded. "That stew won't eat itself."

But Daniel lingered in the barn doorway, his face set in hard lines that reminded James painfully of Michael's expression before delivering bad news. "Dad," he said quietly. "Beth. We need to talk. Now."

"Son, you're exhausted. After you eat."

"Now." Daniel's voice left no room for argument. "What we heard on the road… you need to know."

James caught Beth's slight nod, saw Michael already moving to join them. Even Robbie, usually quick to head home, stayed rooted in place.

"Take everyone inside," James told Sarah. "We'll be there shortly."

Maddie hesitated in the doorway, but Sarah's gentle hand on her shoulder guided her into the house. The screen door's slam felt oddly final.

Daniel waited until they were out of earshot, his voice dropping. "Sherman Masters was on the road with a gang from Portland. They're planning something. Something big." His hands clenched. "And they know about the farm. About Emily treating people. About the supplies."

The evening shadows lengthened as Daniel relayed what he'd overheard, each word landing like stones in James' stomach. He spoke of what they saw in Portland and how Maddie's tale was even worse coming out of Boston. Beth's hand moved instinctively to her weapon, while Michael's posture shifted subtly into combat readiness.

"How many?" Michael's question cut straight to tactical concerns. Heightened anxiety evident in his clipped tone.

"At least a dozen we saw, but they mentioned more." Daniel scrubbed a hand across his face. "They've got military-grade weapons. Talked about 'clearing' Cornish, starting with this farm."

Beth paced a tight circle, gravel crunching under her boots. "We knew Portland gangs were pushing north. Jerry took a bullet proving it." She paused, fixing Daniel with a sharp look. "But Sherman? You're sure?"

"Saw him myself. He's running with them now." Daniel's shoulders sagged slightly. "Almost got us on the Standish road. Had to abandon the truck, carry Jessica through the woods."

"Explains the wheelbarrow," Robbie muttered.

Michael moved to the barn's entrance, scanning the tree line as he spoke. "We need proper patrols. Not just watching the roads - we need to know what's happening in the woods, the old logging trails." He turned back to the group. "I've been thinking about mounted units. Horses don't need fuel, can cover rough terrain."

"The Packard place has horses," Beth said slowly. "Good stock, well-trained. Old Man Packard was a cavalry enthusiast."

"Need riders, too," James added. "People who know the land, can read tracks."

"I can train them." Michael's voice carried quiet authority. "Start with basic horsemanship, work up to patrol patterns. But it'll take time."

"Time we may not have," Daniel interjected. "The way they talked… they're getting organized. Building numbers. And Sherman knows every back road, every deer trail in three counties."

The sunset painted their faces in shades of red and gold as they stood in a tight circle, the weight of Daniel's warning settling over them. From the chicken coop, children's laughter carried on the evening breeze - a stark reminder of what they stood to lose.

"We can't let them get that far," Beth said finally. "We need to be proactive. Set up checkpoints, establish a perimeter." She glanced at Michael. "Start that mounted patrol training immediately, even if it's just basics."

James nodded slowly. "Frank's smoker operation gives us an excuse to have more people around without raising suspicion. Extra hands that could help with defense if needed."

"Frank Wilson?" Daniel's head snapped up. "Since when do we trust---"

"We don't," James cut him off. "But right now, he's useful. And his people are better armed than most."

Michael shifted his stance, something calculating in his

expression. "Could work in our favor. Let Sherman's group think we're just processing meat, not preparing defenses."

"Speaking of preparation," Beth added, "we should talk to Pete's group. They've got that machine shop running on generator power. Might be time to discuss manufacturing more than just replacement parts."

The implications hung heavy in the growing darkness. James watched his son's face, seeing the same bone-deep exhaustion he felt himself. They'd survived the collapse, rebuilt some semblance of community, only to face this new threat.

"There's one other thing," Daniel said, "Maddie has experienced some real trauma. They lost their friend to the river coming out of Portsmouth. Her friend Hannah… She stayed with family in Portland. They will not make it there. I told them to find me if they had to leave. We may need to prepare for that."

"I don't know how we can…" Beth began.

Daniel cut her off. "We may never have made it if it were not for Hannah and her family."

"For now," James said firmly, "you need food and rest. We'll gather everyone tomorrow, make proper plans." He clasped Daniel's shoulder. "You got your family home. Let that be enough for tonight. Hannah and her family will be welcome if they come."

Daniel started to protest, but the barn door creaked open, spilling warm light across the yard. Sarah stood silhouetted in the doorway, hands on her hips in a pose that brooked no argument.

"If you're quite finished plotting," she called out, "that stew's getting cold. And Daniel Thompson, don't think I haven't noticed you favoring that arm. Emily needs to look at it after she's done with Jessica."

James caught Beth's slight smile, saw Michael's tension ease fractionally. They had preparations to make, hard decisions ahead. But for now, there was hot food, family, and the illusion of safety within their farmhouse walls.

Even if they all knew it was just an illusion.

The small coop's hinges creaked as the children burst out into the yard, carefully cradling their egg bounty. "Grandma!" Lily called, her earlier fear forgotten in the excitement of their success. "Look what we found!"

"Six whole eggs," Ethan announced proudly. "And Ryan didn't drop any!"

"Did, too, almost," Sophia teased, but her smile was kind. "Betty tried to peck him." Their laughter and giggles were like music after the things Daniel recounted.

"Inside, all of you," Sarah directed, holding the door wide. "Wash those hands first - yes, you too, Ethan. I saw you petting that chicken."

James turned to Beth and Robbie as they walked across the door yard. "Stay for dinner. Sarah's made enough to feed half the county."

Beth shook her head, though regret flickered across her face. "We should get back. Need to think about what Daniel told us, start planning."

"My parents!" Maddie's voice cracked as she appeared in the doorway, her face pale in the fading light. "I have to go see them. Now. Please."

"After you eat," Beth said firmly. "You're swaying on your feet, and they're not going anywhere." She caught James' eye.

"Maybe we will stay for that meal. Then Robbie and I can take Maddie home properly."

Relief flooded Maddie's face, though anxiety still lined her movements as they filed into the kitchen. The room felt impossibly full—children set up at the small coffee table, each chattering about chickens while Sarah directed traffic between the stove and table, Matthew barely spoke as he helped Elena settle into a chair while Marianne laid out the silverware with practiced efficiency.

Daniel emerged from the barn clinic with Emily, Jessica hobbling between them on makeshift crutches. Her ankle was properly wrapped now, though pain tightened her features.

"Sit, sit," Sarah commanded, already ladling thick stew into bowls. Steam carried the rich scent of beef and vegetables, making James' mouth water. "Maddie, honey, right here next to Elena. Daniel, let Emily look at that arm while I get the biscuits."

"After dinner. Mom. I'm starving and half an hour won't make a lick of difference if I faint from being denied the moment of culinary perfection the mouthwatering scent of this stew foreshadows."

Sarah laughed, and James smiled at Daniel. He always knew how to play his mother like a violin.

James sat back, taking in the familiar rituals of a shared meal that settled over them. Though tension hummed beneath the surface, spoons clinked against bowls, and children's voices mixed with adult murmurs. A sound he feared may fade into memory all too soon, and for just a moment, they could pretend this was just like any other family dinner.

Darkness pressed against the windows as Sarah cleared the last of the bowls, refusing all offers of help. The children had long since succumbed to exhaustion—Lily and Ryan curled together on the old sofa, while Sophia and Ethan dozed in the oversized armchair their grandfather usually claimed.

"We should go," Beth said quietly, her eyes shifting with a nod toward Maddie's increasing agitation. "Get you to your parents before it's fully dark."

Maddie nodded, her fingers twisting Martha's handkerchief. The simple square of fabric seemed to hold all her fears, all her hopes about what awaited at home.

Sarah dried her hands on her apron and pulled Maddie into a fierce hug. "You come right back here if you need anything, understand? Any time, day or night."

"Thank you," Maddie whispered, her voice thick. "For everything."

James noticed how Daniel struggled to his feet, exhaustion evident in every movement. "Dad, I should help with the patrols, the preparations."

"Not tonight," James cut him off gently. "Get some real sleep. Hold your wife. Tomorrow comes soon enough."

Beth and Robbie moved toward the door, but Maddie hesitated. She looked back at the sleeping children, at Jessica propped carefully on the settee, at the family that had carried her through hell to reach this moment. In the lantern light, tears shone in her eyes.

"Go on," Sarah urged, her own voice wavering slightly. "Your parents are waiting."

The screen door closed behind them with a soft thud. James stood looking through the front window, watching the cruiser's headlights cut through the darkness, carrying Maddie toward whatever reunion awaited. The aurora's ethereal light painted everything in strange colors, a reminder that their world had fundamentally changed.

"They'll be back," Sarah said softly, more to herself than anyone else. "All of them. We'll weather this storm together."

James wrapped an arm around his wife, feeling her tremble slightly despite her brave words. In the living room, their grandchildren slept on, unaware of the gathering darkness beyond their sanctuary. Daniel and Jessica had already retreated upstairs, their exhaustion finally claiming victory over fear.

Maddie

Home at last…

THE AURORA RIPPLED ACROSS THE NIGHT SKY, ITS ethereal light filtering through pine branches as Beth's cruiser wound down the darkened streets of Cornish. Maddie pressed her forehead against the cool glass, letting the gentle sway of the car pull her back through memories she'd rather forget.

Grace's final broadcast to an audience of none. Hannah's silhouette growing smaller in South Portland's morning haze. Martha's handkerchief, still carrying the scent of her borrowed sanctuary in Boston.

Each mile marker between there and here held another fragment of who she used to be, scattered like breadcrumbs she could never follow home. The girl who'd toured Harvard, dreaming of future success, felt like a stranger now.

"Which way?" Beth's voice cut through her reverie. "Foster's Hardware, that's on Main Street, right?"

Maddie blinked, forcing herself back to the present. "They don't… we don't live above the store anymore. Moved out to Cumberland Street last spring." She swallowed hard. "The yellow farmhouse, just after the split off of Main."

The cruiser's headlights caught something moving in the tree line—a deer maybe, or just shadows dancing in the aurora's strange light. Robbie's hand moved instinctively to his weapon, but the darkness swallowed whatever had been there.

"Been a while since I checked on that section," Beth said carefully. "Things have been… complicated since the lights went out."

Complicated. The word felt inadequate for everything they'd lost, everything they'd survived. Maddie's fingers found Martha's handkerchief again, tracing the delicate embroidery she could no longer see in the darkness. She didn't even know why the small square of material brought her such comfort, and she knew after seeing all that they'd seen, she'd never see the kind woman again.

The cruiser's wheels crunched on gravel as they turned onto Cumberland Street. As the road dipped on the familiar curve, Maddie felt a surge of unexpected emotions.

Their headlights swept across the yellow farmhouse, and something in Maddie's chest tightened. No lanterns glowed in the windows. No smoke rose from the chimney despite the collection of firewood she could see stacked against the barn.

"Something's not right," Robbie muttered, echoing her unspoken fear.

Beth killed the engine fifty yards from the house, the sudden silence pressing against Maddie's ears. The aurora cast everything in shades of green and purple, making the familiar architecture look alien and wrong.

"Mom?" Maddie called out ash she climbed from the vehicle, her voice catching. "Dad?"

The eerie silence felt bad to her. She was sure something was wrong and glanced at Beth who stepped up beside her.

The porch steps creaked under her feet—a sound that

should have been comforting but now felt like a warning. She reached for the door handle, but Beth's hand caught her arm.

"Wait," Beth whispered. "Let me check first."

The unlocked door was another warning sign that made Maddie's stomach clench. Beth pushed it open slowly, the hinges protesting in the heavy night air.

The smell hit them first. Something sour and wrong that made Robbie curse under his breath. Beth's flashlight beam cut through the darkness, revealing dishes piled in the sink, mail scattered across the floor as if dropped and forgotten.

"Mom?" Maddie tried again, desperate now. "Daddy?"

A weak cough answered from upstairs, followed by a sound that might have been her name.

Maddie bolted for the stairs, but Beth caught her again. "Careful," the chief warned. "We don't know…"

Another cough, then her father's voice, ragged and strange, called out. "Maddie? Baby, don't… don't come up here. We're sick. God, we're so sick…"

The aurora's light filtered through upstairs windows, painting the stairwell in its shifting lights as Maddie's world tilted sideways. She'd survived the collapse of civilization, crossed a burning city, lost friends to violence and water and choice - only to find something worse waiting at journey's end.

"Chief," she whispered, her voice cracking. "Please. Help them."

Beth's flashlight beam caught white-knuckled hands gripping the upstairs railing. Her mother stood swaying at the top of the stairs, nightgown damp with sweat despite the cool night air.

"Mrs. Foster," Beth breathed, already moving forward.

"How long have you been sick?"

"Two… maybe three days?" Her mother's voice sounded wrong - thin and watery. "David's worse. Can't keep anything down. The water…" She stumbled, and Maddie lunged up the stairs to catch her.

Her mother's skin burned against Maddie's palm. "Mom, you're burning up."

"Robbie," Beth's voice carried the sharp edge of command. "Get back to the cruiser. See if you can raise the Thompsons. Tell them we need Emily here. Now."

The sounds from her parents' bedroom made Maddie's heart stutter - harsh, wracking coughs punctuated by the unmistakable sounds of retching. Her father had always seemed invincible, the steady presence behind the hardware store counter, but the man she found curled on sweat-soaked sheets looked impossibly small.

"Sweet girl," he managed between coughs. "You came home."

"Daddy…" Maddie reached for him, but Beth caught her wrist.

"Don't touch him," she ordered. "Either of them. Not until Emily checks…" She turned to Maddie's mother. "The water. You mentioned water. Where have you been getting it?"

"The creek," her mother whispered, leaning heavily against the wall. "When the well pump died… the Creek was so close…"

"Oh God." Beth's flashlight beam caught the collection of buckets by the bedroom window, their contents gleaming innocently in the aurora's light. "The creek that runs past the whole town?"

Maddie's mind raced through implications even as she watched her father curl around another wave of cramping. The creek that wound through Cornish like a thread, connecting properties, where animals grazed and drank, carrying whatever contamination might lurk in its innocent-looking waters.

Boots thundered on the stairs—Robbie returning, his face grim. "Emily's on her way. But Chief… there's reports coming in. Three houses on River Road, similar symptoms. The Shoop family out by the old mill. And Frank Wilson was asking about medicine for stomach trouble earlier..."

The aurora's light painted strange shadows across Beth's face as understanding dawned. This wasn't just about Maddie's family anymore. This was about the entire community they'd fought so hard to preserve.

Her mother slid down the wall, boneless with exhaustion. "I'm sorry," she whispered. "We didn't know… the water looked so clear…"

Maddie stood frozen between her parents, unable to touch either one, watching the nightmare she'd just escaped transform into something perhaps even worse. The sound of Emily's truck rumbling up the road carried on the night air, but Maddie barely heard it over the pounding of her own heart.

They'd survived the darkness. Survived the violence. Survived the collapse of everything they'd known.

But now they faced an enemy they couldn't see, couldn't fight - one that moved through their community as silently as the aurora's light playing across the midnight sky.

The beam of Emily's flashlight swept through the contaminated bedroom as she worked to evaluate them, her movements precise despite the horror of the situation. An IV line snaked from each of her parents' arms, precious fluids dripping steadily through medical tubing.

"Likely waterborne," Emily said, pulling off her gloves with practiced efficiency. "Without proper testing, I can't be certain which pathogen, but the symptoms…" She exchanged a meaningful look with Beth. "This could spread fast. We need to warn people not to drink unfiltered water. They need to at the very least boil it."

The rancid smell seemed to permeate everything—walls, furniture, even the family photos lining the hallway. Maddie's childhood home had become a testament to how quickly illness could transform the familiar into something dangerous.

"The funeral home?" Beth suggested quietly. "Neal & York has space, proper drainage, even some medical equipment from when they did embalming."

Maddie's gasp caught in her throat. "A funeral home?"

"It's actually perfect," Emily assured her, already reaching for fresh gloves. "Clean tile floors, separate rooms, good ventilation. And it's centrally located - we're going to need that when…" She stopped, but the words hung between them unspoken… when others start showing symptoms.

Beth's radio crackled. Michael's voice cut through the static. "Got the generator running at the funeral home. Starting to set up beds. How many should we prepare for?"

The aurora's light caught the sweat beading on her father's forehead as another wave of cramping hit. Her mother's breathing had grown more labored, each inhale a struggle.

"Here," Emily pressed a surgical mask into Maddie's hands, followed by gloves and a bottle of sanitizer. "Clean your hands thoroughly. You can sit with them while we coordinate transport, but don't touch anything without protection. This whole house is contaminated."

Maddie's fingers trembled as she slathered the alcohol based liquid across her hands and pulled on the mask. The latex gloves felt alien against her skin as she sank into the chair between her parents' beds. Her father's hand twitched toward her, but fell short.

"My brave girl," he whispered through cracked lips. "Came all the way home just to find this mess."

"Shh," Maddie soothed, fighting back tears. "Save your strength."

Beth and Emily's voices carried from downstairs, discussing logistics, quarantine procedures, the need to test the creek water. Each word hammered home the reality - this wasn't just about her family anymore. The entire community teetered on the edge of catastrophe.

Through the window, Maddie could see the wide arc of light roll up and shine across the ceiling as more headlights approached. It was Michael's truck returning with whatever supplies they'd been told to grab from the clinic in the Thompson's barn. She couldn't seem to escape the damned aurora, painting everything in surreal colors, as if nature itself was trying to warn them about the invisible threat flowing through their town's waterways.

She cursed it under her breath, now irritated at herself at how she initially thought it was so pretty. "There is nothing beautiful about this."

Her mother stirred, eyes glassy with fever. "We didn't mean to... the water looked so clean..."

"I know, Mom." Maddie's gloved hand hovered near her mother's, unable to offer the comfort of touch. "I know."

The floorboards creaked beneath hurried footsteps downstairs as people prepared for transport. Maddie sat rigid in her chair, watching her parents' chests rise and fall with increasing effort. The IV drips marked time with steady drops, too slow against the rapid progression of whatever ravaged their bodies.

"Maddie," her father's voice came barely above a whisper. His hand trembled as he reached toward her. "My sweet girl..."

"I'm here, Daddy." The surgical mask muffled her words.

"So proud... love you so..." His voice caught, dissolved into a wet, rasping cough. Then another. Then...

Silence.

"Daddy?" The word stuck in her throat as his chest stilled. "No. No, no, no. EMILY!"

Her scream echoed through the contaminated house. Footsteps thundered up the stairs as Maddie lunged for the doorway. Emily burst through, medical bag already open.

"Out!" she ordered, shoving Maddie into the hallway. "Beth, I need you in here!"

Maddie pressed against the wall, watching Emily start compressions. The sickening crack of ribs under desperate pressure mixed with Emily's steady counting. "One, two, three, four..."

Beth appeared with the manual resuscitation bag, fitting it over her father's face. Each squeeze forced air into lungs that no longer worked on their own.

"Damn it, David," Emily grunted between compressions. "Don't you do this. Where's the damn AED when you need one?" Sweat dripped from her forehead despite the cool night air. "Come on, come on..."

Her mother's soft weeping filtered through the mask of illness and fever. The scene before her felt like some terrible dream.

But this was no dream. This was how the world ended - not with the dramatic flash of a solar flare, but with contaminated water and failing hearts and the terrible sound of someone trying to force life back into a body that had finally surrendered.

~

In the hallway, Maddie slid down the wall, Martha's handkerchief pressed against her masked face, watching helplessly as they fought to save her father while the invisible killer flowed silently through their town's veins.

"It is impossible to show why certain things should not utterly destroy and end the human race and story..."

- H.G. Wells

Thank you for reading. Please consider leaving a review.

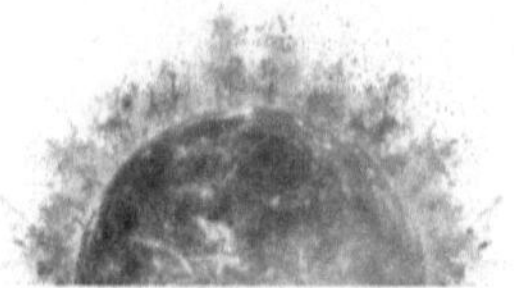

Also by DJ Cooper

<u>Dystopia Series</u>

Beginning of the End

Long Road

Revelations

Dark Days

<u>Apocalypse Fire Series</u>

Endure the Chaos

Survive the Chaos

Beyond the Chaos

<u>Cincinnati Fall Series</u>

Cincinnati Fall 1

Cincinnati Fall 2

Cincinnati Fall 3

<u>Nine Meals From Anarchy Series</u>

Sun's Fury

Terminus State

Insurrection Series

Deception

Evasion

Abolition

WordPeddler Magazines

Acknowledgements

Wasted World is a story of not just survival but of human desire to persevere. The separate journeys through areas mired with challenges around every corner.

What's next for our group in Cornish and what of Hannah? Find these answers and more questions in the next book *Decayed World.* If you would like to stay updated on this and other emerging stories in my new Fire & Ash World, visit my website at https://authoroftheapocalypse.com

I am incredibly grateful to all who read this and my other stories. A passion I never knew existed until I sat down one day to write and now, I try harder with each book, chapter, paragraph and sentence to make it better than the one before. If it were not for the amazing readers who give up their time to walk these tales along with me, I would not be able to do so. It is for you I try to make each one more than the last. I love hearing from readers even if you don't like it. Without feedback I can't do better next time.

I need to express my deepest gratitude to those who were stuck reading this in its early stages. Nancy (N.A.) Broadley is an author friend who is always willing to tell me like it is. Wendy Durison Editor who painstakingly checked that I dotted all my I's and crossed all my T's and didn't use the same word twelve times in a sentence. And I am thankful for Dan Uebel who offers the best insights on many forms of work and is the hard work behind the Book Asylum Podcast. I couldn't do it without your help.